Cascades

General Editor: Geoff Fox

Come to Mecca

Other titles in the *Cascades* series which you might enjoy are:

Talking in Whispers   James Watson
An exciting political thriller, set in Chile under the military junta.
16-year-old Andres Lareta suddenly finds himself on the run from
the security forces. This is the story of his own fight to stay alive
and of the courage displayed by others in the face of tyranny and
oppression.

Fahrenheit 451   Ray Bradbury
This haunting novel centres around a not-too-distant future
where happiness is allocated on a 4-walled TV screen, where
individuals and scholars are outcasts and where books are burned
by a special task-force of firemen. One day, however, Montag,
trained by the state to be a destroyer, throws away his can of
kerosene and begins to read a book.

On the Edge   Compiled by Aidan Chambers
A dramatic collection of eight original short stories from the
thriller genre, including tales of murder, revenge, theft and
dangerous speculation, from authors such as Jan Mark, Vivien
Alcock and Robert Westall.

Come to Mecca
and other stories

Farrukh Dhondy

CollinsEducational
An imprint of HarperCollins*Publishers*

© Farrukh Dhondy, 1978

ISBN   0 00 330089 7

First published in Great Britain by William Collins Sons
and Co Ltd, 1978
Reprinted 1996
Published in *Cascades* in 1993 by CollinsEducational
Printed in Great Britain by Martins the Printers Ltd,
   Berwick on Tweed

CONTENTS

Come to Mecca   9
Two Kinda Truth   27
Iqbal Café   45
Free Dinners   63
Salt on a Snake's Tail   81
Go Play Butterfly   105

FOR Rahim, Khushru, Shafiq and Nosha

COME TO MECCA

Whenever Shahid got angry his short cropped hair seemed to stand up off his head, like the feathers on the neck of a fighting cock. He was very angry that day. When the four of us left the factory and reached the street, he said we should go straight to his uncle's house.

"He will deal with the guv'nor," Shahid said. "I will show that Rasul. Son of a hired woman. When he comes out of the factory I will see him."

"We can't make trouble in the street," I said. "Guv'nor will call the police. Come on."

We went to Masterji's house. We all called Shahid's uncle "Masterji" because back in our village he was the school teacher. Shahid didn't want to waste any more words on us, he walked ahead.

"I don't worry about getting sack. He can keep his bloody job," one of the others said, "there's plenty work. My cousin has a factory. I'll ask him job for you too."

"We're not going to work anywhere," Shahid said, turning his head. "We'll fix this guv'nor first. When I say I'll do a thing, I will die but I'll do it, ask Farid."

Masterji opened the door to us.

"Salaam-aleikum," we each muttered as he let us in.

"As-aleikum-salaam," he said, having fun with the greeting.

Shahid began rattling away in Bengali as soon as we stepped in.

"Wait till you've had a cup of tea. You catching a train?" Masterji said, but as soon as Shahid told him we'd all got the sack and quarrelled with the "bastard" guv'nor, he changed his tone.

"Sit down, start from the beginning, and don't use such words before your elders."

Shahid held his tongue between his teeth in a show of repentance and lightly struck both his cheeks with his palm.

11

He told Masterji the story.

We had all been working at "Nu-Look Fashions". We'd been there for nearly the whole year now, except when the season was out and there was no work. We left school together, Shahid, myself and four other very close mates. Four of us went with the elder brother of another fellow we knew to Nu-Look and he told the gaffer that he'd brought the four machinists he wanted.

The guv'nor took one look at us and knew that we were straight out of school. But that didn't mean we were inexperienced. All of us had done some tailoring for our fathers or mothers at home. Everyone knows machining in the East End. When you are ten years old you begin to forget about being a pilot on Bangladesh Airlines and start thinking of being a cutter or machinist. Of course you usually have to start with just helping out, doing some pressing, fetching Fanta and making tea. This friend of ours told us that there was so much work that this guv'nor would let us start on machines straightaway.

He paid us training wages. After a few weeks we were doing about ten garments a day. He would give us sixty pence for each job we finished, but he wanted us to work faster. The cut cloth was piling up in the corner of the factory and on the guv'nor's desk.

The older workers who sat in the same room were paid sometimes one pound twenty, double what we were getting, but they worked very fast while the Hindi songs played on the cassette all day and the machines hummed with business.

The guv'nor would stand beside Shahid's machine and he would say, "You'll get donkey rates for that, I'll cut you down to fifty pence." First it was a joke. Then he began saying it every day and it became serious, and he'd get angry if we said we wanted to go home when the others went.

"Even a child can work faster," the guv'nor would say.

"I'll get my little sister, then," Shahid would say.

He was not a bad bloke, this guv'nor. He was a white man, but he understood a little Bengali and he'd joke with us all the time and leave us to go to the toilet when we wanted.

"I don't know what you blokes do in there. Where I come from, a piss doesn't take you half an hour."

When a man has worked for sixty pence, he doesn't want to work for fifty. One day the gaffer said he'd been fined for not doing the contract on time, we were ruining his business, we were lazy Bengalis, and the old ones only thought of "taka" (money) and the young ones only thought of "heta" – a dirty word.

Then he said he'd give us fifty for a garment and no more. He was in a filthy mood. Next morning when he let us in, he stopped the four of us at the door and said,

"Look lads, it's fifty pence a garment from today, unless you do more than twenty-five, then it's the old rate."

We sat at our machines. Shahid said to us he wasn't working for one half penny less, not for this gaffer or for his grandfather.

"You can take your cards and clear off," the gaffer said, "you should clean the streets, you can take your time doing that." At the end of that day he went to the drawer where he kept his ledger, and reaching inside his coat pocket took out his fat wallet and peeled off some notes for the four of us.

"That'll be for the last two days," he said, "sixty pence a garment. Not from tomorrow, though."

The next day we turned up to work as usual. Shahid told us to wait near our machines but not to start work. We stood with our arms folded just inside the door of the one-room factory.

"Clear off, lads, I've made other arrangements. If you won't work for new rates there's others as will," the gaffer said and carried on with his own work, walking round the other machinists and filling his ledgers with scribbles.

For two hours we just stood there. Then the gaffer went out for his sandwich and his beer, which one of us usually went down to the street and fetched for him. Shahid addressed the other workers in Bengali. One of them said they'd taken a cut in rates too and then they all dipped their heads down into their work, ashamed.

Shahid said he was only sixteen years old but he knew liars from truth-tellers. He said they were not men and should wear bangles and sarees and stay at home.

The guv'nor came back with Rasul, an old Bengali with sly eyes whom we all knew. The two of them pushed past us and the guv'nor showed Rasul to Shahid's machine. Rasul sat on the stool.

"So you've come to put your foot on my stomach, eh Rasul?" Shahid challenged.

Rasul sheepishly picked up the cloth that Shahid had been working at and started to put it through the machine.

"Don't talk so big when you're only a chit of a boy," Rasul replied.

"I have more pride in my chin than you have in your white beard. Only orphans work for fifty pence," Shahid said.

"I work for what I can get. When you have three children you'll stop going to the pub with your money and going with rubbish white girls," Rasul said, still working away.

"Like your mother," Shahid replied.

"Clear off, that's enough of you," the guv'nor said.

If I hadn't pulled him out of the factory, Shahid would have beaten Rasul there and then.

"I'll see you outside," he shouted, and Rasul just laughed.

Masterji listened carefully to the story.

"That Rasul is the son of a sow," Shahid said.

Masterji put on his coat and we went together to the factory for lunch-time. When the other workers came out, Masterji spoke to them. That evening we all met at Masterji's house. He had persuaded three of the older workers to come. Masterji said we had to call a strike at the factory otherwise this guv'nor would get away with murder. We didn't come to this country to be slaves.

"The others won't listen to us," one of the older workers said. "You all know what Bengalis are like."

"Don't talk about Bengalis to me," Masterji said. "Don't talk about our countrymen in front of me like that."

"Look at that Rasul," Shahid said, "I'll kill him."

"You won't kill the disease, you'll kill the germs that cause the disease," Masterji said.

There was a lot of interest in our strike. The next day we went outside the factory with Bengali placards saying "PAY US FAIR RATES".

One by one the other workers decided to join us, especially after a crowd gathered on the pavement and we began shouting. On the second day of the strike the guv'nor called the police because not one person went to work. The police came and then newspapers came. On the third day one of the older workers came to us with Masterji. We were still standing on the pavement and a lot of our friends had come to support us. This man said he had to go back to work. His wife was in hospital and he was heavily in debt. Masterji told us that he had a fair case, we should not stop him going back to work. He should be allowed to go back till the end of the week at least so he could be paid on Friday. Shahid was sulky but he didn't contradict Masterji. On Friday we knew what would happen. The workers would want to get their two days' pay for that week. One by one they all went back and began to work. The guv'nor came to the first-floor

15

window of the factory and shouted at us. We didn't reply. By the afternoon there were only the four of us left.

It was that afternoon that Betty and Sylvia came to the door of the factory. We saw these two white girls coming down from Aldgate end, carrying a camera. They stopped and asked us if we were the "comrades on strike".

"It's not a strike," I said. "We've just stopped working till the guv'nor changes his mind."

They wrote down everything we told them and then Betty took a photograph of us. We all brushed our hair and they asked us to lift up the placards even though we didn't want to be in the photograph with placards in Bengali. We put our arms round each other's shoulders and stood under the "Nu-Look" sign. Betty went with the camera and knelt down in the street. All the traffic had to stop as she took her photographs, but she behaved as though she didn't even notice the horns and the shouts from the obstructed cars.

"Cheeky woman," Shahid said to me in Bengali.

Some days later we were sitting in one of the cafés on Brick Lane drinking tea. All the boys who are out of work hang around the five or six cafés there and drink endless cups of tea and wait to hear of any jobs that might be going. We knew that the season was over and even experienced men couldn't get much work. Betty walked into the café and she seemed to recognize us. She came over to our table. At first we didn't recognize her. The day she took the photographs she'd been wearing jeans and a leather jacket and a sweater with a black fist on it. Now she was in a dress and her hair looked as though she'd washed it and brushed it just for us.

"I've been looking for you," she said to Shahid. "We've written you up magnificently."

Then she put the pile of newspapers she was holding on to the table and began turning the pages.

16

Now white girls rarely come into that café, and if they come they are with their men. Only rubbish women sit in the café all day and go with men who make friends with them and pay them. Bengali girls never come to that kind of place. Some Ugandan people come, and some stylish Punjabi girls, but they are allowed to have boyfriends who bring them. They are decent girls and nobody says anything to them. Betty was a decent girl too, she had a good accent, but like other white girls she didn't know how to behave, where to go and where not to go. She went anywhere she liked and did what she liked and nobody said anything to her.

We didn't want to insult her so we asked her if she would like to have coffee and we told her to sit at a different table from us, because the boys we were with were just staring at her and grinning. They were third-class, good-for-nothing rascals, but we were sitting with them because they were telling us how to buy and sell cars for plenty money. Betty motioned to them to push up and sat at our table. There we were in the photograph. The newspaper said "Workers Fight Blacklegs in Sweatshops". Shahid was not sure of what it said so he asked Betty to read it to him.

"No blacks in that factory," Shahid said to her, "only Bengalis."

"It's black*legs*," Betty explained, "people who attack workers."

"If anybody attacks me I will punch them," Shahid said.

The others in the café were now curious and gathered round the newspapers. The papers were passed from hand to hand.

We told Betty that the strike was finished and she said that it was a shame.

"I'm not ashamed," Shahid replied. Then Betty told us that she worked for the newspaper and she started selling the

17

paper to anyone who would buy it for five pence.

"Anyway," she said to Shahid, "I'd like to talk to you. We want a whole story on the sweatshops."

"We don't know much stories, only Bengali stories," I said.

"About your sweatshops, your factories, Nu-Look."

Shahid looked puzzled so Betty said, "We call them sweat-shops because the labour is sweated labour." She was anxious to explain.

"When I sweat I always take bath, not like English people."

"You've got me wrong. The factories are filthy and dingy, all of this area."

"My cousin's factory is very clean," I said.

"You must be joking," Betty said, "I've seen some of them."

"He never jokes with ladies," Shahid said.

After leaving the café that day we went to Shahid's house. Shahid told me not to mention the paper and he screwed it up tight and put it in his shirt because he said that if his father saw it he would say that it was giving Bengalis a bad name. We sat all evening watching telly at Shahid's house. That was the kind of mood that came over us when we were out of work. Sometimes we went to the cinema on Commercial Road and then came back and watched more telly. When we had money we went to the West End.

All the boys told lies about their adventures in the West End. A fellow would be sitting in the café and he'd tell us how he'd been to a gambling casino and won fifty pounds on the gaming tables, or how he'd gone to a dance hall in Leicester Square and picked up two beautiful white girls who were really decent girls, and they really fancied him because of his hair-style and he could do anything with them whenever he liked. When we were still in school we believed these stories and waited for the day when we could go out, go dancing, get some girl-friends. You live and learn. When Shahid and I went to the West End we had our own fun, but no one talked to us except to pick a fight. We'd go on the bus and then we'd play the pinball machines and see some sex films and eat ice-cream and take the last tube back to Aldgate or walk home if it was too late or if all our money was finished, first along the river and then through the echoing stone walls of the City streets.

We were aimless, at least Shahid was aimless until Betty discovered us. Shahid had met her on the street again, he said, and he had made an appointment with her to go to her house with me.

"You're fixed up," I said, grinning, but he turned savagely on me.

"She's a good girl," he said, "she's educated, not like you."

"Her father will take one look at both of us and kick us down the street."

"These kind of girls don't have fathers," he said, thoughtfully.

"Her brothers, then."

"Just shut your mouth and come with me."

We went the next day. We sat on the floor in her strange room. She didn't even have a settee, and her bed was just one mattress on the floor, like a villager. There were hundreds of books all over the place. Everyone who came to her room sat on the floor on cushions amongst all the books and tea-mugs and papers. Even the light was hanging down from the ceiling nearly to the floor with a paper bowl on it, and there were coloured candles which had spread pools of wax on the furniture.

She told us that she was a translator and showed us some Russian books and French books and Shahid asked her to say something in French and in Russian, and she said it and we all laughed. When he asked her what that meant, she said, "It means 'I love you' " and we all laughed again, and she could see that Shahid thought she was saying it to him, so she said, "It's the easiest thing to say in any language."

Then I said it for her in Bengali and Shahid said it in Urdu like they say it in the pictures and she tried to learn the Urdu.

Whenever we went there, Betty talked about the strike we had been in, but after the first time there was nothing new to tell her. She told us that we were not only part of the Bengalis but also we were part of the working class and we should forget about being Bengalis only. So I said I'd always be a Bengali and Shahid told me that I didn't understand what she was trying to say.

"Working class are third-class people," I said. Betty tried to explain that we had learnt all that from the newspapers who were against workers.

Betty liked explaining those sorts of things. She would talk very slowly so we wouldn't have to say "pardon". It seemed to me that Shahid loved listening to her voice, even though I'm sure he didn't understand half the things she was saying.

I only went there because Shahid kept wanting to go back. Betty said we had told her very useful things about Asian life and then she began telling us about her political party. She was part of a political party and it wasn't secret, anybody could join.

"You are a communist?" Shahid asked.

"Well, I'm a socialist. All workers should be socialists and trade unionists. It's the only way working people can lift their heads up. Communism comes after that."

"Communists are no good," I said, "they blow up railway trains in India."

20

"You are ignorant," Shahid said. "You know Maulana Bhashani, he's a communist. Has he ever blown up a train?"

"He's a saint," I said.

"And you are a simpleton. Masterji said he's a communist."

Betty was very pleased when Shahid agreed to go to the meetings. He told her that I would have to come too. She had light grey eyes and Shahid said that her eyes were like a cat's, and she asked us if we thought cats were beautiful.

Shahid said he thought they were very beautiful and they also caught rats.

When she was alone with us Betty talked a lot, but she didn't say much in her group meetings. When we went to the first one with her, it was in a row of houses which had been taken over by people just like hippies. At each meeting there were about a dozen people in the room. A bearded man was their leader. He always spoke second, waiting for someone else to start him off. Shahid asked Betty if he was the president, but she said they didn't need a president, he was only very clever and very active. At the first meeting the leader asked her to tell the meeting about the Nu-Look strike and she told them and we agreed with everything she said. Then the bearded man talked straight at us and said we had to get into a union if we were going to win. Someone else explained that we could start talking to Bengalis about joining the unions and we should go back to Nu-Look and persuade everybody to join the union. Everyone in the room said that was right and Betty nodded her head and said she should have thought of it first. On the way home Shahid became very sullen and he said that he didn't trust Bengalis, they wouldn't pay any money to join anything. Then he said he didn't trust the man with the beard, the leader. I said I was never going back to Nu-Look even if they paid me a

21

thousand pounds for each coat.

The next time we went to Betty's house the bearded man with the checked trousers was there. Betty didn't chat with us as she usually did and I could see that Shahid was disappointed. Instead, she told us that they were making plans to get all the workers into their party and we must help because we were Bengalis. Then the bearded man started giving us a lecture and walked up and down the room. Shahid didn't want to listen, so he said he had to go to Hessel Street for his mother. Betty said we should listen and after we'd finished the discussion she wanted to do some shopping too. The leader said that we weren't fighting the Nu-Look manager, but we were fighting his whole system. He said the police were on the side of the manager, and the government too, and that even the government of Bangladesh was on the side of the manager.

"Do you like China?" Shahid asked.

"We have theoretical disagreements with the Chinese Party," the man said, impatient at being interrupted.

"So you don't like China? My uncle likes China," Shahid persisted.

"We disagree with their theory of social imperialism. Look what they did in Chile."

Shahid didn't know about that, he said, but added that his uncle had lots of books on China, more books than there were in that room even, but they were all in Bangladesh. If he wanted, Shahid said, his uncle would lend him some books and he could read them and maybe he'd understand a little more. He said this defiantly to the man and the man turned to Betty and said, "It's useless, I don't know how to reply to that."

Betty could see that I was uncomfortable because now Shahid was getting angry with the man.

There was a silence and Shahid and I got up to go. Betty

walked to the door with us.

"Roger's just a bit impatient," she said. "He's brilliant really. You'll get used to him as you start working with us."

Then she did something she'd not done before. She reached out and held Shahid's hand. She was looking at him and smiling to let him know that she wanted to talk to us too, and to drink coffee and laugh as we usually did, and that she was sorry it had turned serious with Roger there.

"You have to come to the next meeting," she said. "It's really very important. We'll get you organized then. We'll train you to understand all the theory. You must join the group properly, I really want you to." She winked.

As he walked away, Shahid seemed suddenly happy. He lifted the hand she had held, elegantly to his nose, as though to keep the fragrance of her with him. I didn't say anything. There was nothing to say.

When we were in school together, we had known some rubbish white girls, but we never went to their homes. We'd meet them in the cafés and play Hindi love songs for them on the juke-box, "Kabhi-Kabhi" or any nonsense song of the time, and we'd play pinball machines with them and they might let you kiss them once or twice if you could overcome your own shyness. We hadn't known any girls like Betty before.

"Do you like that girl Sylvia, Betty's mate?" Shahid asked me. I didn't like that. It was as though he was trying to make me beg him for favours.

At the next meeting Betty didn't sit with us. She sat next to the leader because she was giving a speech. She got to her feet and talked about fighting the National Front and then something about Jews and about "Asians". When she talked to us she said "Bengalis", but when she made speeches she said "Asians". She abused the National Front for selling newspapers. The rest laughed when she said

23

filthy words. I could see that Shahid admired her for being able to swear in public. He said afterwards that when girls like Betty used filthy language it was all right, it wasn't lowering their family name, it just meant that she had very strong emotions against rubbish people who attacked Asians.

After that meeting he tried to ask her if he could go round to her place, but she said to him that she had to go now, but he should definitely make it a point to come round before the meeting of the group on Saturday. Shahid said that it was a signal. I shouldn't go with him this time. He said she'd asked him to go alone. I understood.

For three days I didn't see Shahid. He was working at a friend's factory, I heard, to pick up some quick money. On Saturday the meeting was supposed to start at two o'clock. I didn't want to go. I had gone to be by my brother's side, because Shahid was like a brother to me, but you don't always want to be "kavab me haddi", the "bone in the kebab", someone who gets in the way.

I sat in our usual café from about ten that morning. About eleven o'clock Shahid came in, his hair looking as though it was flaring out of his head. He was wearing a new suit, blue with pin-stripes, and a new shirt with its huge collar covering the jacket lapels. I could tell from the way his mouth remained slightly opened, his thick lips parted, that things hadn't gone as he had expected. In his right arm he was carrying a whole pack of newspapers.

"Come with me," he demanded, looking around the café to see if anyone else was staring at him.

"You getting married?" the manager asked him, mockingly.

"Why should I, when I get your wife and daughter free?" Shahid said as we walked out.

24

"What's the rush, where are we going?"

"They gave me these," he said, thrusting the wad of newspapers at me.

"You've had your picture taken again?"

He was in no mood for mucking about.

"I have to sell them to 'Asians'," he said.

"Wasn't she there?"

"She was there. They were all there. She called me before the meeting because she said I was ready to help the group with its work. They gather at her place before Saturday meetings to sell newspapers."

"Where are we going to sell them?"

"Tower Bridge."

He was angry and walking fast.

"There are none of our people on Tower Bridge, only tourists."

"Sometimes seagulls," Shahid replied, tight-lipped.

"Where have you been all these days?" I said trying to get him to talk to me.

"Saving money like a fool," he said.

We walked on past the Aldgate roundabout and turned down Alie Street.

"I asked her to go to Mecca with me," he said finally.

"So you got somewhere, what're you so furious about?"

"I followed her to the kitchen where she was making coffee for all of them. I said will you come to Mecca with me. She's so stupid, she thought I meant Mecca in Arabia and said she wasn't a Muslim and what did I believe in religion for, because religion was like drugs. So I told her I meant Mecca Dancing, this evening, later tonight. She thought I was messing about."

"Did she say she'd go with you? Do you want her to be your girl-friend?"

Shahid didn't reply. We had reached Tower Bridge. He

took the newspapers which I had been holding. The headline said "Fight Nazi Front".

We walked down the bridge and when we got to half-way between the two great trunks of the bridge with the water swirling round the curved stone, he threw the whole pile of papers over the grey railings on to the fast water of the high tide.

"What the hell are you doing? Police will catch us for throwing litter about!"

We walked back to the café. We drank some coffee and talked to some of our friends about the football fixture between The Welfare Team and Navin Sangh that was to take place on the Vallance Road field that afternoon at two o'clock.

We were lost in our talk when Betty walked into the café with Sylvia. She came straight up to us, her arms draped with her own pile of newspapers.

"Where's your lot, Shahid?" she asked. "You can't have got rid of them already!"

Shahid looked up at her, pretending to be very off-hand.

"Oh yeah," he said, "I got rid of the lot."

"That's great," she said, "fantastic. Now we can really make an impact on blacks. Start with the Asian community."

She was smiling and she and Sylvia exchanged looks.

"You must have worked very hard and fast," she said to Shahid.

Shahid pulled out his wallet. He held out a couple of pounds to her. "I have to pay you off," he said. "That's for the papers."

TWO KINDA TRUTH

My name is Irving, but they call me Clyde on account of my friend Bonny. Bonny and I used to go together from the time we knew almost nothing. You could say we grew together. We went to the same primary school and then to the same big school and we always met after, and on Saturdays we washed cars down the street together and split the breads we made from that and from anything else. We weren't like twins, because I was like Bonny's shadow. I even caught my name off him. The youth them, they started to call us Bonny and Clyde after we were accused of doing the same robbery. The name stuck, even though the charge of robbery didn't. We got off because this smart lawyer . . . but that's another story, yes?

Bonny, boy, he grew smarter than any of the youth we used to hang around with. The first day we moved to this dread school in Battersea, he takes one look around the place and says, "It soft. Man could be happy here." Now, looking back on it, I don't know how we could have made such a mistake. That school was split up in three. There was the main building, all new and still being built, where they kept the smart ones. They were all white and one or two Asian kids and a couple of blacks. We were kept in what we called the "coal heap". It was down in Wandsworth and we called it that because there was a whole heap of coal in the yard. The teachers, they called it the "Annexe". There was only a few whites up there, most of the youths on the heap was black.

We stayed in that place three years before we was moved and had to come up to the main building because it was complete and the heap was shut forever. Before that we only saw the main building when the coaches fetched us to carol services or some other jive occasion and the headmaster would stand up and do he thing.

Anyway, this story's not about that school and about

blacks and whites, because it would have to be longer than the longest book anybody so far writ. This story's about Wordsy and Bonny. Wordsy was a teacher. He wasn't called "Wordsy" at all – that was the name Bonny gave him. He was an English teacher. No, first he was a student guy, one of the people who come and waste your time because they're training to be teachers and they need guinea-pigs. We met him, all those years ago, in our English class. Old man Cottage usually came in and gave us some spelling test or told us to read "The English Way Reader, Book I, II or III". But this day here, Wordsy come through the door. He was carrying a handbag on his shoulder. He was a young guy with long hair, kinda hippy. He walk in cool, cool, and say to us that Mr Cottage was going to come down and introduce him, but he was a man believe in his own introduction.

Most of the youth just mucked about in that place. We never listened to nobody. We just didn't want to know. When we got to know Wordsy, years later, he told us that he was nervous that first time, like really shaking. He'd never been in a class before and he was not even sure that he should have been teaching. And we told him that he shouldn't have brought his handbag with him. He should've suss the place and come with a briefcase or something.

As soon as the youth saw the handbag they began to shout "butty, butty, butty man". Of course Wordsy didn't twig what they were calling him. He wanted some quiet, so he rapped on the teacher's desk and stood up straight to show that we couldn't mess with him. But nobody would listen. It was like that; we always tested out the newcomers. Then Wordsy tried getting hold of one of the youth in the front and tried to reason with him.

Bonny just watched him careful. Then he said, "Hush your clamour and let the man speak." That's how Bonny talked, always a bit fancy. They called him a wordsman. Immediately, Wordsy saw that Bonny was some kinda leader in that mob, so he turned to him.

Then Bonny stood up and turned to the class and started bowing and making a little speech and everyone turned to watch him and laugh. He pretended he was mucking about, but really he was getting everyone's attention, helping Wordsy along.

"All right, now that you're quiet, we can start," Wordsy said, but even Bonny's effect didn't last long and the others started throwing things at the man. He just sink down in the teacher's chair and say he'll sit there till it quiet.

"You'll have to be bury in that chair, sir," Bonny said. "It never going to be quiet, we ain't quiet for nobody."

As the class went on Wordsy got desperate. He'd brought some papers along and me and Bonny walked up to his desk and asked him what he'd got there. He showed us. It was some poem by a man called Wordsworth and Bonny asked him if he'd writ it himself. The man say that he wish all his life he had writ it, but he hadn't.

"You got the copyright, then?" Bonny asked, just to be feisty. Then he shouted to the class that the man was called Wordsworth and he was no ordinary man here, he was a PO-YET. The class wasn't interested. Bonny looked at the sheet and said, "Hmm, it all right," and Wordsy smiled, but he was nearly crying before the bell went and he'd wasted the whole lesson.

Two days later, when we'd all forgotten the guy, he comes back. English was in the afternoon and it was in a classroom just by this heap of coal, looking out on the yard. The room had huge windows, like doors almost. When he come in, the whole class cheered.

Bonny nudged me with his elbow because he had a key to the doors of all the rooms in that place and he indicated to

31

me that we should lock the door so that Wordsy wouldn't be able to get out. The man was trying to smile. In the confusion, Bonny slipped over to the door and locked it up.

"You see I haven't given up with you," Wordsy told the class.

"What's your name?" they were asking.

"Never mind my name. Let's get down to some reading," he said and he distributed the papers straight away. He began to read as soon as the papers had reached our desks.

" 'Let us go then, you and I,' " he read.

"I ain't going nowhere with you," someone shouted.

"Are you really a butty, sir?"

"This man drunk," one of the boys in the front row shouted.

"To tell you the truth," Wordsy said, "to face you lot, one has to be either drunk or superhuman or mad. And since I can't induce the oblivion of madness, and since God made me painfully mortal, I've had what we call a little nip, as weakness shall be my witness."

"Your breath smell foul, sir," the boy in the front said.

"Talk fancy again," Bonny said. "This guy's good, you's a preacher man like old Cottage."

Bonny always appreciated that sort of style. Cottage would talk a bit like the Bible, you know, a bit of high talk. "Do unto thy brethren as they would do unto you. Betray them. Grass them up," he'd say, and then he'd say, "Put your hands on your hearts, remember your Maker and confess to throwing chunks of coal through the staff-room window, or I'll flog the lot of you."

The youth liked that. Cottage kept order with the cane, and with little tricks like that. He'd talk grand and then he'd talk cockney all of a sudden and it make everyone laugh, but it make them scared at the same time.

Wordsy read his poem after that, and he got the hiccups

and some boys rushed over and started hitting him on the back, saying they'd make his hiccups go away. By the time the lesson was finished, Bonny was saying to me, "This man all right." I could see that Bonny liked the way he was talking, using big words, laying it on when he found the class silent for a moment. Bonny was fascinated by words even then. If we went to a blues, he'd listen to the new lyrics and dub tunes and try and learn the rough bits and change them here and there and use them himself in his speech.

By the time the bell went the youth were waiting to see how Wordsy would get out of the room. They all knew the door was locked. He tried the door. Then the boys crowded round him and asked him if they could see his handbag, and if he had a boy-friend and all kind of rudeness. Wordsy was desperate to get out. He crossed over to the big windows and tried to open one. It was jammed shut. The school-keeper had nailed it down to keep kids from running out of that classroom. Wordsy didn't see the nails and he just banged on the catch harder and harder till he missed, and his fist went clean through the window, smashing the glass.

"That's school property," someone shouted.

It wasn't a joke. The glass had cut right through Wordsy's wrist and the blood was pouring out. Wordsy fell to the floor saying, "Oh my God," and holding his wrist, his eyes wide with disbelief.

Bonny pushed the others aside and went up and knelt by him. There was going to be trouble now, we could all smell it. The joke had gone too far.

"Go sit down," Bonny motioned to the rest and they did as he said.

"Mr Wordsworth," Bonny said and the student man looked up. There were tears in his eyes and still the blood flowed. "Shall I call Mr Cottage?"

The man shook his head. The class was dead silent now.

"Gimme hanky," Bonny shouted.

Someone gave him a coloured hanky and he tied it round the man's wrist. Wordsy looked finished, boy, he couldn't even kneel straight, he was going to topple over.

"Go get Cottage," Bonny said to me, holding the man upright.

"Mr Wordsworth, hang on there, guy, we fetching somebody."

Wordsy shook his head.

"My breath," he said, "drink. Don't call Cottage."

Bonny understood. He got the key out of his desk and rushed up to the staff room to call the young drama teacher. He was thinking right. She was also a bit hip, like Wordsy, and she wouldn't grass him up. She came down and took him away.

We didn't see Wordsy again till we'd nearly finished with the main school. I was in the sixth form. Bonny left at the end of the fifth, telling the head that he wanted to look a job. He didn't look a work. He just came back when he got fed up of lounging about and told the sixth-year master that he had been discriminated against and all the jobs always went to the white boys and all this, and they sympathized with him and let him back into the sixth form, even though he hadn't been bothered to take any CSE or O levels or nothing.

Bonny told the head that he was interested in maths because he could get some technical training after, but we knew that he wasn't really. He was just interested in relax. He joined the English class because I was there. I'd done my O levels and I was going on to do A level English. I was interested in it. I liked reading books. When Wordsy reappeared and started doing his kind of thing, English became more interesting. In a way even Bonny admitted that Wordsy was good.

Wordsy came back as a teacher this time. He didn't look much older to us.

"Where did I check you before?" Bonny said, strolling up to him in the sixth-form room. "I see you before somewhere, Jah."

"You tell me," Wordsy said.

"You was a bouncer in the Stalawart Club up in Islington, right?" Bonny grinned, "and you call the Babylon when things get too hot for yuh to handle, right? And the youth swore revenge as they drag him off to prison to do some heavy pieces. But now I break loose of the dread calaboose and I come for my revenge." Bonny stretched two fingers out in a mock gun.

Wordsy caught on fast. He raised his hands and said, "You may have shot the Sheriff, but you mustn't shoot the deputy."

"Nice, nice, nice," Bonny said, "you all right?"

"Have I seen you before?" Wordsy asked, narrowing his eyes.

"You still owe me one hanky, for bandage your hand," Bonny reminded him.

"Of course," Wordsy said with real wonder and astonishment and respect, "of course. You know when I came in this morning I asked some of the staff if the old three-ten were still around and they said, 'Yes, some of them.' What they meant really was, 'God send the plagues to try us instead of these pupils.' How are you?"

Bonny was never in Wordsy's class, but Wordsy would let him come and sit in on lessons.

"Not for the work," Bonny would say, "I like being with my *spa* Clyde." But Wordsy could see that when we were discussing poetry or reading it in class, Bonny's attention was just there. Bonny and I had never split up really. Even during the term he was off school and I was doing exams, I'd see him a few evenings a week. He began to move with a new crowd, but I tagged along with them and we went to the "Centre" in the evenings. A whole posse of youth hung out there. It was supposed to be a youth club, so two nights a week there were sounds, and sometimes guys hired the place and brought in Coxson and Sofrano B and the big boys. The rest of the time, the Centre was boredom and hustle. Guys would sell weed and just use it as a meeting place for play ping-pong and dominoes, and drift in and out of the Judo class which was run twice a week by a Japanee man.

Though Bonny had made some kind of mark, even there, he was just a swordfish with a lot of sharks around. Maybe that was why he wanted to come back to school. He'd got some sort of reputation as a dread man. Not that Bonny is heavy or heavy-looking. He's thin as a whip, but fast, you know, real fast. And he could talk. He'd got in with a gang of youth who ran a sound system called "Kool Skank", and when they were playing at the Centre, Bonny would take the mike and play DJ. He'd carry on a whole rap in front of the music, imitating Big Youth and Jah Stitch and Dr Almantado. He was building himself a small reputation as a real dub artist, a man whose toasting was really hot.

That was the time Wordsy started his poetry circle. He'd done some writing himself and he always boasted that he had friends who'd written real books and poems. I said I was interested and so did Bonny. On Wednesday nights we'd stay after school, and several girls from the English set would stay behind too and Wordsy would give us some sherry to drink and we'd go up the staff room when nobody was there and start the sessions with him reading some poetry. That was his little trip. He'd read some T. S. Eliot and then some guy called Hopkins which was like Rasta poetry about God and thing. Bonny said, "They all sound

36

like West Indians, them poets, with names like Gerard and Wystan and Dylan."

He'd ask Wordsy some funny questions, but really honest. He would ask, "How man could learn hard words?" or he'd ask, "Could you lend me a book with all the rhyming words in English inside?"

Wordsy didn't like them kind of questions, but he'd try and answer them serious.

"Don't obsess yourself with impressing people," he'd say. "A poem doesn't have to rhyme. Rhyme is a sort of escapism."

"Rhyme is musi-kal," Bonny would reply.

"Well, it depends," Wordsy would argue. "A poem has to have its own internal music, something more convincing than rhyme." Then he'd leaf through the books piled by his chair and say, "You hear that? It seems to have the whole rhythm of speech."

"I ain't speak like that," Bonny would say. "You don't speak like that either. Find me a man who talk so. Poetry is not natural talk. If you talk like that on the street man will think you mad."

Wordsy would fend off the arguments. "You have to be a little mad to write with inspiration. Poets, drunkards, mad-men, you know what Shakespeare said about lovers . . ."

Bonny was impatient with Shakespeare. He'd ask if Wordsy had managed to sell any of his poems. The others would get shifty, and yet they enjoyed the sort of interruptions that Bonny would offer.

Wordsy would say no, he hadn't sold none, but success was a bitch goddess, it was not what a poet should be after. A poet should work like a carpenter, finding the right-sized nail, shaping the right joints between his thoughts.

"And between him fingers," Bonny would say, "are true, are true, are true. You sight it?"

Wordsy's stuff made some sense to me because you have to learn all that to get through A level, but Bonny said it made no sense to him, it was all failure-talk. Sometimes the girls would bring their poems and read them aloud to the circle. Wordsy would sit back, biting his lip and pretending to think hard about the words. Bonny would watch him. The poems were all about high-rise flats and how depressing they were and about loneliness and old people on park benches and shit.

"Methers again," Bonny would say and look at me.

One day Bonny brought his own poems. He'd kept them a secret. Only now and then he dropped me a hint that he was going to be a great poet.

"Hold on there," Bonny said as the session started. "I and I have something here I want to present to the attention of this circle."

Wordsy was pleased. He always wanted other people to read before he dragged out his own typed stuff.

Bonny took his floppy cap off and lifted the sheets from under it. The girls laughed.

"This one come straight out of my head," he said.

This was the poem:

All across the nation
Black man suffer aggravation
Babylon face us with iration
Man must reach some desperation.
It have to be iron, brothers y'all, it have to be iron, my sisters.

Babylon hold up the power
Black man reach the final hour
Our strength in Jah is like a tower
Bringing down a merciless shower
Of bitter rain, my brothers y'all, of bitter rain, my sisters.

He read the verses with tremendous seriousness. The others listened and, as he read, their eyes darted to Wordsy, who was sitting with his head in his hands and his elbows perched on his knees.

Bonny finished and met with absolute silence.

"What's wrong with it?" he asked aggressively.

"Oh, nothing, nothing in the least," Wordsy said. "It's fine, just one or two things, a couple of small points."

The rest of us didn't say nothing. We were in Wordsy's English class and we knew that when he didn't approve of somebody's work he'd say, "Fine, fine, a couple of points," and then he'd launch in for the kill.

"Don't dig no horrors," Bonny said. "No big thing, say what you like."

I knew that there was a certain amount of defiance in Bonny's voice. It was like an unsureness. He'd stuck his neck out and now he was going to protect it, but he had to know where the attack was coming from.

"I can, or at least I *think* I can appreciate what you're trying to say."

"Deaf don't even hear thunder," Bonny said, quickly.

"Quite, quite," Wordsy said, licking his lips which had gone dry. He was pulling some determination out of himself. "Yet it seems like you've thrown together a lot of words without much thought."

"I think all the time, you don't need a degree to think."

"For God's sake, I'm not saying . . ." Wordsy trailed off. "Well, all right, I'll give it to you straight. I think there's a lot of rhyme there, but there's no poetry, if you see what I mean. I don't mean to be discouraging, your sound patterns certainly show you've absorbed something, but there's no personal emotion. The poem is too much of a slogan; to be poetry it has to have the sound, not of propaganda but of, well, how shall I put it, of *truth*."

Bonny screwed up his face. He put the poem back under his maroon velvet cap.

"Yeah?" he asked. He was hurt. He kissed his teeth.

"But we can ask the others. We should get more opinions," Wordsy said. The girls were embarrassed, either by Bonny's righteous, strong poem, or by Wordsy's reaction.

"All right," Bonny said. "It cool. But remember," and he got up to leave and turned round as he was leaving, "remember, Mr Wordsworth, that there's *two* kinda truth."

"There was no need for that," Wordsy said after he'd gone. "No need for anyone to take criticism so personally. If you're a writer, your work is public property, it's not your little toy . . ."

There were no more poetry sessions. The circle was closed.

Bonny didn't appear in the English lessons the next day. Then he dropped away from school. Wordsy seemed tense and nervous in those days. He never mentioned Bonny to me and he stopped calling me Clyde. He started calling me "Irving" and I stopped calling him "Mr Wordsworth". Bonny disappeared from school. Once, when the sixth-form master asked Wordsy in front of the rest of us whether he'd seen Bonny, Wordsy said, "Humankind cannot bear too much reality". And that was all.

Just before my exams I started going down the Centre again. I recognized some of the faces and began getting back into it. The poetry circle hadn't been cancelled, it had just faded away. So one Wednesday evening I was down the Centre and the poster outside said: "The Immortal and Versatile Sounds of Kool Skank, Hosted and Toasted by the Byron of Brixton, Bonny Lee". I smiled to myself, because I knew who Byron was, but most of them youth, them wouldn't know. It just sounded good. The sounds were in the usual hall. The lights were turned down and the amplifier turned up and a jam of bodies presented itself as I went in.

For half an hour the music played, and Bonny's voice introduced the discs with a flourish. "The latest creation of the Jamaican nation . . ." etc.

The bodies undulated. There was a thick smell of ganja about the room. "Strike while the weed is hot . . ." Bonny shouted over the mike and he was greeted with catcalls and approving shouts. "Go on, boy, fire some heavy shots, dread words 'pon the waves." Then all of a sudden the record faded with a scratching sound. Some of the sounds-men gathered round the turntables with torches and began to put it right. "Hold on there, hold a stool and keep your cool, brothers and sisters," Bonny's voice announced over the mike. "The emergency disco have hit an emergency in itself."

The crowd was restless. They waited for a few minutes and then in the darkness they began to shout. They were threatening a stampede.

"Record player bust to boomber," someone shouted.

The youth workers charged down from their office when they heard the commotion. They worked their way to the sounds table. There was an argument going on. The turntable had stopped functioning and the sounds-men were trying to figure it out, but the crowd wanted its sounds or it wanted its money back.

Then Bonny's voice came over the mike again. He was reciting some verses. They were his own verses and he read with a sort of threatening solemnity. Gradually the noise of the crowd, its protest, died down. People were listening.

"More," they shouted when he'd finished his first poem.

Bonny went through another, his voice reaching a higher pitch with excitement. Now the crowd was listening spellbound. "Of bitter rain, my brothers y'all, of bitter rain, my sisters," Bonny declared.

Then the record player was fixed and Bonny's début as a

41

real poet was over. But when the record came on, the crowd shouted for more poetry. When the first record was over, another voice introduced Bonny again and a third and fourth and fifth poem boomed out over the amplifier.

After the session, Bonny waded his way through the crowd to the door. He saw me. He was sweating and his face shone with wet elation.

"I like it," I said.

"Wha' go on there, Clyde?" he said.

"I there," I replied and smiled.

Bonny and I stood outside the club and we talked of school and we talked of Wordsy. Bonny laughed and gave me a message for him.

I didn't give Wordsy the message. Then the day I was leaving school a black girl in the sixth form brought in a poster and pinned it to the notice board. It said: "BONNY 'BYRON' LEE", and it announced a poetry session by the "Poet in Residence" at the Lambeth Library. There was a paragraph explaining that "Byron" Lee had been given a grant by the Arts Council to work at "black poetry and literature".

Wordsy came into the room and his eye fell on the poster. "So our friend Bonny's a professional poet," he said to me.

"It would seem so," I said.

"Do you ever see him?"

I told him I had and then, because he'd brought it up, I gave him Bonny's message.

"We was talking about you as a matter of fact," I said, "and he told me to tell you that he was wrong. That there aren't two kinds of truth. There's only one: Truth is what the masses like."

"Hmm, that may be, that may very well be . . ." Wordsy said.

"But listen, he also said to thank you very much for being his teacher and showing him the ropes of poetry, Wordsworth and Eliot and Byron and all. He said he's been reading Wordsworth."

"He didn't, did he?" Wordsy said, his eyes lighting up.

"Yeah, that's what he said," I lied.

IQBAL CAFÉ

n Wednesday afternoons the café served fish, Bangla-style, and Clive always found it crowded with Bengalis. There was not only the usual young crowd who hung around the café day in and day out, but crews of older Bengali workers who only came for the fish. Clive knew he could pick up leads for several stories from the café. He would have to wait for the business to subside and go in late in the afternoon. Hoshiar Miah, the proprietor, whom the boys called "Langda Miah", "the lame one", would always drop him the hint of a story. Some of the boys he knew would fill him in on the goings-on around Brick Lane. He'd pick up things other reporters couldn't get. He had become the *East London Herald*'s Asian specialist, and half his work was done in the Iqbal Café.

When he first acquainted himself with the Iqbal Café, hardly any whites went there. Only two or three regulars. There was "old Annie" who'd walk in with seven or eight carrier bags, place them in the corner and walk up to the counter to ask Langda Miah for a small loan to have a coffee in his café. Langda knew her, the boys knew her. They would start calling out, "Hello, darling," and the bolder ones would make vulgar kissing sounds on their palms and some would ask how much she was charging nowadays. It was a routine. She would turn to them and swear in Bengali. It was said that she'd been married to an Indian once, and he'd left her and that she'd been through two world wars, and had entertained gentlemen of all the races in the world. Langda would give her a free coffee provided she didn't make an appearance more than two or three times a week.

Langda had been at pains to explain to Clive that his name wasn't Langda at all, that it was Hoshiar Miah, "the clever one". Clive remembered this and always called him by his correct name. The lads didn't seem to care. They called him

47

"bionic" sometimes, because he was lame in one foot, wore it in iron clips and in a huge padded boot which he dragged after the other leg as he walked, leaning on a stick or on the tables as he passed them.

"I like you always coming," Langda invariably said to Clive. "It is good to talk with intelligence people."

His remark was directed at the two young men who were at the far table slopping up curry with a shared plate of chapattis.

"Teach him something," one of the boys said. "As he grows older his hair is falling out and his brain is in his hair like Samson."

"Of course Mr Clive can teaching something. He is journalist. They knows lots things."

"What things do they know?" Clive asked. "You've told me everything I know, Hoshiar Sahab."

"Don't talk with these puppies, Mr Clive," Langda said. "Leaves them. They don't even know to read and write. Stupid as donkeys." One of the young men looked up, provoked.

"You are the donkey. We saw you carrying two rice sack on your back."

When they were teasing him, Langda always addressed his remarks to them through Clive.

"You know how hard it is for business these days," Langda said. "I tell you, Mr Clive, why a boss man have to carry he own rice. This boy here, you see, I bought his grandfather for slave, now he sick and complain he can't work."

"He don't want buy trolley, Mr Clive. Always carrying rice on his own back like donkey."

"Leave them, crazy peoples," Langda said, bringing Clive his curry and rice and a cup of tea and sitting down opposite him at the table.

"I want you to give one thing in your paper."

"What's that?"

"It is Iqbal birthday."

"He want to advertise his dirty restaurant," one of the young men said. "When you write it, tell the public that Langda was fine hundred pound for cockroach in the rice when the inspector come."

"This is a friend of yours, this Iqbal?"

"Mr Clive, why you joke with an old man? It is Iqbal's birthday. That's why I name my restaurant Iqbal Café. The greatest poet in Persia, India, Pakistan, Bangladesh, Burma and Ceylon. I don't know about China and England."

"How old will he be?"

"He dead."

"A centenary?"

"Whatever you like," Langda said, thinking Clive had agreed to run the story. "If you like you can write that the famous restaurant is name after famous poet. When I first came Brick Lane I saw all the stupid peoples and I'm thinking this restaurant must giving some knowledge, some beautiful."

"You should change the name after the Bangladesh war. Iqbal is a Pakistani poet," said the young man who'd been silent so far.

"These boys not understand poetry," Langda confided, leaning forward, then turning to them. "Why you doesn't only see Bengali film, why you see Indian film, Paki film? See? now the boy can't answer. I like Urdu poet. Most sweetest language in the world, just next to Bengali and English. Iqbal, Tagore, Nazrul, Shakespeare, all artists, all brothers."

Clive could see that he was glowing with sentiment, probably recalling some favourite verse in his head.

"He is a traitor, this Langda," the young man said. "He

never have Bengali name or picture or anything. Look what he prefers. Naked white ladies." He pointed to the prints that Langda Miah had recently put up on the wall to raise the tone of the place. There was a huge print of "Déjeuner Sur l'Herbe" with a nude sitting in the midst of a lot of well-dressed nineteenth-century men.

"Too much dirty mind. You know how he lose his leg, Mr Clive? They cut it off for going with other man's wife."

"Oi, shut your mouth and have respect for elders," Langda said to the boy.

The two had finished eating and went in turn to the basin at the back of the long narrow room and washed their hands. They were about sixteen or seventeen years old. Under their shiny black, well-styled hair, they gave off a sense of assurance, a sense of smiling confidence. One of them, whose name Clive knew was Rafiq, was a sort of leader. He had high cheekbones and the faintest suggestion of slant eyes, some throwback to East Asian ancestry. When ten of them were gathered together, he'd set the pace, tell them when to go, when to pay, how to set the style of teasing Langda that day. And he was the best-dressed one among them. Most of them wore flared Terylene trousers, open-necked shirts and checked jackets. Rafiq wore blue suède trousers, a denim jacket and pointed boots.

Langda wore baggy trousers and a faded navy blazer. Since Clive had been there, he had heard a hundred different versions of how Langda lost his leg. Langda Miah's own version was the most heroic. Several times he had told the story in Clive's presence, sometimes in Bengali, sometimes in Urdu, sometimes in English. Each time it was somewhat different. It was always heroic, but the odds stacked against the hero, himself, changed.

The leg had been shot off by dacoits in his village when he

was the only man who would stand up to them to prevent the women of the village being raped. They had raided at night with shotguns. In one version they were disguised policemen, in another version they were Indian spies, in another version they were hirelings of the landlord. In all the versions, Hoshiar Miah had stood firm against them. He had gone out with his bare hands and taken on six of them, killed two and had his leg shot off in the battle. He had driven them away from the village. The whole band had retreated before his single-handed defence, and the village was so grateful that his wife and children would never go hungry. He had left them in Bangladesh and the village would feed them in perpetuity.

Langda limped up to the picture the young man had pointed out, and pretended to adjust its position.

"He call *me* dirty mind. *I* don't go with rubbish girls," he said.

"You saying you saw me with rubbish girls?" Rafiq asked, pausing behind Langda. "If you saw me then you must have apricots instead of eyes," he added in Urdu.

"I will tell you about these boys sometimes, Mr Clive. They think they are too big now, their heads become swollen with politics."

"So they should be," Clive said. He wasn't getting much news this afternoon, but as it wore on, there were bound to be more young men coming in with gossip of some sort.

"Some mens come to the Bangladesh Welfare Association and call all these boys and they go like little sheeps following its mother for milk. A big Jamaican leader, he come and say everybodies must do fighting. What these boys knows about fighting? They comes from between mother's legs yesterday."

"Ai, Bionic, don't go on mothers. You say anything about

mothers and I'll break your other leg."

"Now they all want fight, but don't know how, Mr Clive. In Bangladesh is too much fighting. First British, then Pakistani and always dacoits. This boys is cowardness, can't fight, no bottles. The white people in East End very rubbish people. If this boys makes troubles, *phuta-phut* going to finish them off. Scared inside itself." He touched his heart and grinned at Clive.

"This same boys, Rafiq and Mushtaq and Altaf and that black-faced Hussain," Langda said, "the police catch them in car with iron bar, milk bottle, big wood stick. Look for trouble. No good." He shook his head.

Clive remembered the incident. A few months earlier some of the young men who hung around the Iqbal had been nabbed by the police for running what the newspapers had called "vigilante groups". When he interviewed them after their release from the police station, three of them had told him that the police had slapped them and roughed them up and told them to "piss off back to Pakiland".

"We has to defence ourself," one of the young men had said to Clive. "Too much white peoples coming and attack Bengali for nothing."

"I reported the case," Clive said, recalling the wrangle that he'd had with the editor who refused to allow him to publish anything but the bare facts of the arrests.

"You should be support for us instead of complain to Mr Clive," Rafiq said.

"If you want to thrash Paki-bashers, you should thrash them, not going round in car and looking girls."

"We were looking for the white gang who beat up Mushtaq Ali."

"Now he say this! In Magistrate Court in Old Street, he begin beg. 'I was going to evening college with friends',"

Langda rose from his seat and began mimicking, putting on a whimpering voice. "Then magistrate say 'Why you carry milk bottle?' so this boy here who is too much big liar say his mother wanting some milk. So much lie. Talk politics in Iqbal, tell lie in Old Street."

"Don't shout it all over Brick Lane," the boy said.

"Mr Clive, this boy Rafiq. Big leader, eh? One day he sitting where you sitting now and making joke with me and a Punjabi boys comes in. Six peoples. They sit down and Rafiq start his insulting, so the Punjabi boys gives him one tight slap. So this boy bring three other boy. These Bengali boy all think they is big expert of fighting. So Punjabi boy pull out a dagger and stick it in the table and Rafiq just make shitting his pants, gone home."

"When was this?" Clive said. He looked at Rafiq. It was obvious from his expression that Langda's story was essentially true. Rafiq looked worried.

"Don't worry. Mr Clive is a reporter, not a police," Langda said, going behind the counter now to take the boys' money.

"These boys don't know what fighting is. When I was Bangladesh, during the war, lot of soldiers come and shoot. Then we has to fight. No one afraid, everyone like lion."

"He telling lies, Mr Clive. When the war was going on he was in Leamington Spa, working in factory."

Now Langda changed tack. He felt he'd pressed the lads to the point of retaliation.

"You call him 'Mr Clive'. Oi, boy, do you know what that name is?"

"It's the name of a reporter."

"It's the name of your conqueror, you fool boy."

"Is he in National Front?" Rafiq asked.

"No, I'm not in the National Front, he's just bein

frivolous," Clive said.

"Didn't Clive conquering Bengal and this boy's great-grandfather?"

"*Your* great-grandfather, or whatever, too," Clive said.

The boys didn't understand.

"You see, they have no knowledge of history," Langda said.

"Clive was the name of the first Paki-basher," Clive said, but it didn't seem to leave the young men any the wiser.

The boys paid and left, and Langda smirked.

Clive decided he wouldn't wait and gossip with Langda. He had to rush back to the office and file a housing story before the secretaries went home. He got into the office car and drove down the one-way of Brick Lane, under the brewery causeway, under the bridge and down towards Bethnal Green Road. The corner of Brick Lane and Bethnal Green Road was deserted on Wednesdays. On Sunday, in the morning, there was a market there. It was where the fascists sold their newspapers, spitting and swearing at the unwitting Asian shoppers who passed. Clive had attempted to report some of the skirmishes that took place, but the editor had dismissed them as minor incidents not worthy of notice. He'd told Clive that he'd had enough of petty assault cases. Clive hadn't had enough and he thought that the editor was a racialist and a mug.

The Iqbal was just one of Clive's haunts. Sometimes in the afternoon or in his own time in the evenings, he would walk into a pub where known members of the National Front, or other fascists, met. He knew them and they knew him, and _____ a lukewarm welcome. The articles which _____ his name constantly sided with Asians in _____ s and the like, and once or twice he'd _____ e bitter attacks on racialists. And yet the _____ ather or The Clock and Orange wouldn't confront him directly, wouldn't goad him into a serious argument. Some one of them would always say "Watcha, Clive, old cock," and buy him a pint and slip him the hint of a story.

Though Sunday was Clive's day off, he normally put in a few hours of investigation. He woke up late that Sunday and regretted it when he finally got down to Brick Lane, parking his car at Aldgate and beginning to walk the length of it. There were police cars everywhere. The street was full of constables.

"Some trouble?" he asked, going up to one he knew, putting on his reporter's manner.

"Trouble at the other end."

"Come on, Handley, be more specific, what sort of trouble?"

The copper smiled and looked away, pretending to be bored. "That's for me to sort out and you to find out."

No use wasting time on this sergeant. The higher-ups would be more forthcoming. They understood about press–police relations. This fellow was a punk anyway, Clive thought. They were all racialists, these junior coppers.

He walked briskly down the street. The Bengali shops, even those that stayed open on Sundays, had closed down. There was a kind of hush in Brick Lane. Clive looked at his watch. The market must have folded by now; it was past one o'clock.

There was a crowd of young men outside the Naz cinema and further down on the left, by the mosque, a group of older men in long black coats and black caps had gathered. They all seemed to be looking down towards the other end of the lane. Clive walked to the Iqbal. Six young Asian men stood outside. They looked him up and down. Two of them he recognized and said "Hello" to, and they in turn said something to the others in Bengali. Clive didn't like the tension in the atmosphere. Even the ones who'd greeted him didn't have that edge of normal exaggerated politeness, the "Hello Mr Clive, how are you" tone. They simply nodded, sullenly. Behind this group of young men, Clive saw something new. One of the big plate-glass windows of the Iqbal had been plastered over with a huge portrait of the Queen, with a Jubilee announcement below it. It covered all but two feet of the six-foot-tall glass. Clive was mildly amused. As far as he could recall, there had been a small poster of some Indian actress, with her breasts bulging improbably out of her swimming costume, stuck on the inside of that window. He vaguely remembered that there had been some banter about it between the young men and Langda Miah.

The café was darker with the huge Jubilee poster shutting out the light. Clive noticed immediately, on going through the door, that the poster had been stuck outside to cover the shattered glass of the shop window. There was no evidence of mayhem, but the glass of the window had clearly been smashed and the splintered edges which remained removed hurriedly, leaving a few jagged seams in the frame.

"Hello, Mr Clive," Langda Miah said. "Fish only Wednesday."

Clive pulled out his shorthand pad and pen from his sheepskin coat. He stood with his weight on one leg, holding the book, deciding to abandon the slow, chatty approach when he saw the faces in the crowded café look up at him as though he were an intruder and not wanted.

"Hoshiar Sahab, tell me what happened."

"Sit down and have a coffee. It is nice to talk with educated peoples."

Langda was clearing up the left-over cups, limping from the tables to the counter. The two young boys who did the waiting for him, carrying balanced plates of curry and trays of rice and chapattis from the kitchen to the tables, stood idly at the counter. Hardly anyone had ordered a meal. They were there for the shelter, it seemed.

"Tell me what's going on here. What happened to your window?"

"I'm advertising for the Queen. She is good lady," Langda said. There was a hush in the café. Normally at that hour on a Sunday there'd have been a flare of noise. Clive would have joined any one of the groups of young men he vaguely knew. He'd listen to their talk about factions, how someone was for the pro-Bangladesh and someone for the pro-Pakistan lobby. They'd tell him stories about Langda, about how he'd tried to cheat his partner when he owned a tailoring shop, or about how he had offered to help them set up a Bengali Youth Arts Club because he desperately wanted to be elected as its president.

Taking in the scene, Clive decided that he'd address his questions to Langda. "Who smashed your glass?" he asked. Langda was behind the counter making him a coffee.

"No one smashed the glass, I'm advertising. Not enough money in tea and coffee business. This boys is not eating curry nowadays, their stomach full with politics."

"Mr Clive," Rafiq called from a table at the back of the café. Clive knew from the tone that it wasn't an invitation to sit down, to have a coffee and a chat. Clive turned to Rafiq. He looked two feet taller. He had a bleeding scar on his left cheek. His forehead had been cut open and was dabbed with toilet paper.

"Rafiq, what the hell is going on?"

Rafiq didn't seem interested in answering the question. He was looking at Langda as he spoke.

"What you say to a man who's scared of the sound of his own footstep?"

"Is this the news you came for?" Langda Miah asked.

57

"The hero of Bangladesh," Rafiq said. The only sound that followed was the clump of Langda's foot as he dragged it along the floor, fetching Clive's coffee. His face was drawn, weary. He wasn't going to exchange any banter with Clive. He looked as though he was thinking about some distant event. "We win it, Mr Clive," Rafiq said. Clive began to understand. They were all waiting. There must have been twenty-five young men there, and as Clive looked from one face to the other, he was reminded of a scene in a film in which American GIs were waiting to be flown out to take a parachute jump into the middle of enemy territory.

"Tell me all of it," Clive said. As he looked around he saw more scarred faces. There had been a battle. There were a few torn shirts and ruffled hair in evidence. Clive looked across at Rafiq. He leaned over Rafiq's table, placing his hands on it. The young men at the table didn't look up at him. One of them said something to the others in Bengali. They didn't reply. None of them were making an effort to make him feel comfortable, Clive thought.

"They did a lot of damage?" Clive asked Rafiq.

Rafiq said something in Bengali, raising his voice as though addressing all the young men in the café. Then he turned to Clive.

"No. We beat them good. Teddy boy or something like this. Come in twenty-five from the National Front market. They beats up one Bengali boy and send him to hospital. Ambulance come in half-hour. Afraz Miah was shouting from the street and we was in here and in the other café and then we all comes out. Lot of Bengali men, young men, coming out and then when mosque finish, they all behind and in front of the Teddy boys. We beat them good. Seven almost dead on the pavement. Ten, fifteen run away and start throw brick and then more Bengali boys come and beat them to the ground. One white boy get glass in the back of his neck. Police come and catch ten Bengali and two white and the ambulance pick up the rest of the white. They tear Rahim shirt off his back."

As Rafiq told the tale, his chest expanded with a kind of pride. "They will come back with more," he said. "They say they come back with guns."

"My God," Clive said. "Look, there are cops outside, the place is lousy with them."

There was a titter in the restaurant. Clive felt suddenly self-conscious.

"You live long time in East End, Mr Clive," Rafiq said. It was clear to Clive that he was addressing everyone in the restaurant now through him. "The police is joining National Front, coming on the side of anyone who is attacking Asians."

"Yeah, yeah, I sense that," Clive said. He looked round at the faces that were looking up at him.

"You might be knowing it," Rafiq continued. "You are writing story in the newspaper. You are knowing for writing. We are knowing for living."

Some of the young men smiled. Clive felt himself shuffling from foot to foot. "Maybe some publicity will help. It'll expose these people, get the police to move instead of brushing it under the carpet," Clive said. As soon as he'd said it, he wished the words back in his mouth. None of them there would believe that the newspapers would do them a blind bit of good. Clive had the uncomfortable feeling that he didn't believe it himself.

"Newspaper never go against police," one of the young men near the door said. Rafiq gave him a reply in Bengali and then turned to Clive.

"It don't matter. You writing a good story, Mr Clive."

59

Clive could see that Rafiq had sensed his discomfort and was patronizing him out of some Asian sense of politeness. Slowly the café came alive in talk. It was all in Bengali. Clive wanted to tell them that he was on their side, that maybe in some small way he could help, but he remained silent. He felt he couldn't leave the café either. Their eyes would follow him. It would be something of an admission, like saying to them that he understood that they were reluctant to trust any white man. It would be admitting that he had suddenly begun to feel like a scavenger, moving in for news whenever he picked up the scent of a kill.

"And some people too scared of these dacoits," Rafiq said in English. His tone had turned challenging. "Write one last story in your paper. All Bengalis not stay together like white peoples. Some is too much scared."

Maybe that was Rafiq's way of saying that he'd finished with him, Clive thought. On some previous day, he would have been sitting opposite Rafiq and the statement would have been part of the testing banter, an opening gambit for an argument. The young men seemed to approve of Rafiq's words and his tone. He was rallying them. So maybe the Iqbal Café had finished with him, Clive thought. No more fish curries on Wednesdays.

"This boys always make up big, big story, Mr Clive," Langda said, breaking the silence. "When this Rafiq went to court, they gave him swearing to do. He hold up the card." Langda Miah stood before Clive and self-consciously began again to act the scene out. "They hold up card, but the boy can't read. He go to school and thinking only one thing, about dirty girls. Don't learn read or write. Then judge say him, 'Swear by Allah', and he say he swear by Allah, but he don't know what he swearing. The boy don't know British rules and British peoples. He don't know what to say."

"When they smash his window, Bionic didn't know what to say. He run to kitchen, phone up police: 'Yes, this is your friend, Langda Miah, Inspector, you coming quick, bringing lot of police and take all fighting boys away?'" Rafiq rejoined.

"These boys' foolishness bring all trouble on whole Bengali community," Langda said, but he sounded defeated. He turned and limped back towards the counter.

"When the National Front come up the road, he was hiding in his kitchen and begging police. He say he shot hundred dacoits. I tell you he got his leg cut off for going with women. My uncle told me."

"Look, Mr Clive," Langda said, turning to Clive, who was still standing in the centre of the room. "These boys eat my bread and they coming on me. I am a poor man. I have only this one shop . . ."

"He come out and try and stop the fighting," one of the boys at Rafiq's table said.

"They want a lame man to help with some kicking," Langda said. His face was taut.

"Who is cowardness now?" Rafiq asked.

"Look, Mr Clive, look," Langda said, and he lifted the hem of his trousers to reveal his shrivelled leg strapped into shafts of steel in the boot. "Allah gave me this leg. These boys bring me some blame. What it is I can do?"

"Why you come into Brick Lane, then?" Rafiq asked.

"Allah gave me this leg," Langda muttered. He turned to the counter. He walked behind it and hesitated at the door of the kitchen, turning to face his clientele again.

"If you want politics you come to Brick Lane," Rafiq said, a sort of cruel delight in the discomfiture of the lame man overtaking his face, "and if you want business, you go elsewhere."

61

"All right, I'll go other place, is plenty place," Langda said. Clive turned to go to the door. The Iqbal was closed to him.

"God gave me birth with such a leg, otherwise I would have fought with these boys, kick Frontwallah in the face," Langda said, as Clive opened the door to leave.

FREE DINNERS

orraine was in my first-year class at school and the only reason I noticed her was because she was on free dinners like me. We was the only two in that class who had to take the shame of it. We had a right nasty teacher, Mr Cobb, (so you know what we used to call him). Just the way he called your name at the end of the register made you crawl and feel two feet small. He'd collect the money from the other kids and make Lorraine and me queue up separately at his table. Not that he ever said anything to us. He just finished with the regular kids and then announced "Free Dinners" even though there was only two of us.

After the first week of that, I couldn't take it no more, so I used to go and sit in the bogs when the dinner register was taken and go down to the office after and get my mark. That was dangerous too, 'cos when some wally set fire to the bogs, I got the blame. The register never seemed to bother Lorraine. She would stand up in front of me, and even at that age she looked unconcerned with the way the world treated her. She had a look of thinking about something else all the time, and had tight little lips which showed you that she was right tough and determined – and she was skinny as barbed wire.

She was a coloured kid, or at least she was a half-caste or something like that. We always called them "coloured" when I first went to school because we didn't think there was nothing wrong with it; but after, some of them would thump you if you called them "coloured". They didn't like that, they wanted to be called "black". I'm not really sure to this day what she was, on account of never seeing her mum or dad. All the other kids would talk about their mums and dads and the gear they had indoors, but Lorraine always kept herself to herself. She wasn't much to look at and she didn't get on with any of the other girls, because some of the white girls were right snobbish. The other coloured kids would talk black when the teachers weren't there, and they left Lorraine out because she never.

She was good at sports and she was good at drama. I wouldn't have noticed her, I tell you, because at that age I wasn't interested in girls. The other lads would talk about what they done with girls and that, but I couldn't be bothered, and because I was skint till the fourth year, I never took no girls out or even let the kids in the class know who I fancied. It was a girl in our class called Wendy. She had a nasty tongue, but I liked her. I remember the first time Lorraine and I stood in the free dinner queue, Wendy said, "She looks like she needs them and all." The other kids laughed, and I must have blushed all over my fat cheeks. Old Cobblers didn't tell Wendy off or have a go at her, and Lorraine just pretended she didn't hear.

I kind of hated Lorraine. I knew that the rest of the class thought that we was tramps. I knew it wasn't her fault, but she was kind of showing me up just by her existence. She wouldn't go and hide in the girls' bogs, she'd just stand there in front of Cobblers' desk and be the only one in the class on free dinners, and because she was there the other kids would know I was hiding, because Cobblers would say, "Biggs has gone underground again," or something.

When Lorraine started coming flash the other kids began to take notice of her. In our fifth year she was going to get the drama prize. She was good at acting, and the drama teacher had sent her to some competition which she'd won. She dressed her up as a page boy and gave her a boy's part from Shakespeare. It made her look nice, because she had short hair and sort of squarey shoulders, even though she was as thin as a broomstick. I was the captain of the football team and had to pick up the cup for the team on prize day. The deputy head called all the kids who'd won prizes into the hall and told us that the Bishop would be there to give us our prizes that evening and how we should make sure that our parents came. She went on and on about school uniform and what the boys should wear and how we should wash our hair and have clean hands for the Bishop to shake. Then she turned to the girls and did a right turn, showing them how to curtsy, which made them giggle. Then she goes, "I've told you this before, but I'll rehearse it with you again. You won't be allowed to accept any prize unless you're decently dressed, and that means school uniform. If you don't have one, you'll have to get a skirt below the knee, a clean white blouse and blue cardigan. And no blue and green tights. I want all the girls to wear flesh-coloured tights."

"Whose flesh, miss?" Lorraine asked.

The deputy head stopped as though Lorraine had clocked her one. Some of the girls giggled.

"Go and wait outside the hall for me, will you, Lorraine?" she said quietly, and Lorraine walked out, saying, "I only asked a simple question," and she knew that at least a few admiring eyes were following her.

It was the first time I had heard Lorraine say anything coloured, anything to show that she knew she was coloured. I'll tell you straight up, that if anyone else had said that, I would have thought it was too flash. The coloured kids in our year were a load of wankers. They didn't want to mix with the rest of us. When they had a laugh it was on their own, and they collected together in the fifth-year room at lunch times and after school and took over the record player and just played their dub and reggae and that. Some of them were all right, but some of them just liked to come flash with you.

When we gathered that evening in room B12, behind the stage, waiting to get the prizes, Lorraine walked in looking a real state. She had on black velvet hot-pants and a black silk shirt and had made herself up to look right tarty with crimson lipstick and heavy eyeshadow. The girls sort of turned away when she came in and the boys started making remarks and whistling to take the piss and I was looking, just staring at her because she didn't half look different, dressed like that. Then the deputy came in and threw a fit. Her jaw dropped down to her tits. She rushed Lorraine out of the room and we all ran to the door to hear them arguing in the corridor.

The deputy was telling her that she could still get her prize if she'd wash her face and change into a spare skirt and blouse that she'd give her. But Lorraine wasn't having it. It was as if she'd turned beastly at sunset or something. She gave the deputy some nasty cheek and the deputy didn't turn the other one, she just tried to tell her to "clear off the premises", and Lorraine said she'd wear what she liked out of school time because it was her culture, and the deputy said she was still in school time if she was inside the gates. When the deputy came back in our room, she was sort of blinking to hold back her tears, looking like Lorraine had really told her which stop to get off at. Lorraine didn't collect the prize of course.

It was after that prize day that Lorraine became a bit of a loud mouth. I heard her telling some of the coloured kids that the deputy head was jealous of her and prejudiced, and didn't want her to be an actress, and wanted to shove her off to work in a laundry. And Lorraine took her revenge.

We were in the maths class and the deputy came in and put her coffee mug, which she always carried around the corridors of the school, down on the teacher's desk. She asked the teacher's permission and began telling us about some fight on a bus in which our kids had duffed up the conductor or something. Everyone was listening quietly and Lorraine, pretending to talk to another girl, said, "I bet she'll blame the blacks." The deputy didn't pay any attention, just finished what she was saying and then asked the maths teacher if she could have a word with him outside. She was a bit put out, so she left her coffee on the desk and went out with him.

When they stepped out, Lorraine got up from her desk and went to the front of the class and looked in the coffee cup. We thought she'd take a drink and some kids said, "Go on, dare you." So Lorraine turns to the class and says,

"What, drink *her* coffee, and get rabies?" and she cleared her throat with a loud hawking sound and gobbed into the cup, a huge slimy gob. She stirred it with her pencil and without a smile to the rest of the class, sat down again. The two teachers came back in the room and the deputy took her coffee and split. The maths geezer said that Lorraine was to report to the Head's office at 12.30. Lorraine said, "Yes, sir," and the maths feller said, "You ought to be given a taste of your own rudeness." The kids all laughed and he didn't know why.

It was at that time I think that I began to admire Lorraine. I told myself that if I got the chance I'd ask her out, but I didn't want any of the lads to know what was on my mind because, for one, they didn't ever take black girls out, not the mob I moved with in school and, for another, they thought Lorraine was some kind of looney loner. That's why I didn't ask her to the fifth-year dance, and good job I didn't, because she came to the dance with a group of black boys from Brixton and they pushed past the teachers at the door and began to act like they owned the place. I think Lorraine just brought them to show that she moved with the dread locks or whatever they liked to call themselves. It wasn't going to be a particularly good party with no booze or nothing.

These kids brought their own records and they broke up the dance when they started threatening the guy who was playing DJ for the evening. The guy stopped the music and the teachers switched all the bright lights on and suddenly the place was full of teachers and schoolkeepers, and when Lorraine's crowd started arguing back, they called the police. A lot of the white kids began to drift off, because a blind man could see there was going to be trouble.

I was watching Lorraine. She looked as though she knew she had gone too far. She was trying to cool it and reason with her black friends, but they shoved her aside and shaped up like they were going to duff up the DJ. Then someone said the police had arrived outside and the black kids legged it. Lorraine got into a lot of trouble on account of that scene. Some of the kids, the next day, the white kids, were talking as though they were scared of Lorraine. The blacks were laughing about it. Lorraine wasn't laughing with them; she was just pretending she hadn't been there and getting on with her classwork. That's what I liked about her. She created hell and behaved as though she was the angel of the morning.

At this time I was going out with Wendy. She was right hard, harder than a gob-stopper, and she always settled arguments with her fists. I suppose I was a bit fed up of her really. She never let me touch her all the time we was going out. She was a bit of a tom-boy and didn't even want to be kissed. Her dad was a copper and strict. I had to take Wendy home at eleven even if we went to a party. I was fair sick of her, even though she was a good-looker, nice face, big tits and always dressed flash.

I wanted to ask Lorraine out and I knew that Wendy would do her nut if she found out. I brought up the subject once with the lads I used to circulate with, and they figured that Lorraine was right easy, that she'd let you do anything

70

with her. They said the black guys from Brixton whom she went out with wouldn't hang around her for nothing. They figured she wouldn't go out with a white bloke. I didn't say nothing to them, but one day after school when I knew she had drama club, I waited around in the year-room and played records till the other kids had gone home and started chatting her up.

I was quite surprised when she said she'd go to the pictures with me. We fixed it for the next time she was staying late at school. I didn't tell the lads in school about our date, but I phoned my friend Tony, who lived in his own flat and told him that I might drop in for a bit after the pictures if my bird fancied staying out. I had six quid on me that day. I met Lorraine up the Elephant in the evening and I said I wanted to go to the Swedish movies, they were really good, but she laughed at me and took me to some crummy film about some stripper girl in Germany or some place.

Lorraine didn't talk silly like Wendy. She had sort of two sides to her. She was a bit posh and she was also hard black. She'd go to the pictures that snobs would see, and she'd want to go to plays and things, and then she'd also talk rude and swear in Jamaican and that.

Until I took her out, I never knew she talked so much. She was explaining the film to me. It was nice listening to her. She wasn't thick like Wendy. When she started explaining why the stripper done what she done, it was nice. It was like I'd had six pints and all the words made sense to me, or like I didn't care if they made sense or not, there was something new and exciting about them.

Then after the pictures I asked her if she fancied going down to my friend's place, because he might be having a party and she gave me a smile and said she was hungry.

"Fancy some chips?" I asked.

"I'm going to take you out to a meal, Peter," she said.

71

That touched me. It fair knocked me out, to tell you the truth. We went to this Chinese joint she knew in the West End. She was putting on the style, but I didn't mind.

When we sat down they brought this tea that smelt like bad after-shave. She started pouring it out and knocking it back and I said I couldn't drink tea without milk and three teaspoons of sugar and she laughed.

"What do you want to eat, Pete?" she asked. "Don't worry, I'll pay."

"I'll have a plaice and chips," I said, not looking at the menu.

"Don't be so thick, 'darling'," she said, pronouncing the 'darling' like one of the girls in the film we'd just seen.

"Steak and chips, then," I said.

"You can stop playing Cockney hero now," she said.

"I ain't eating no ying yang food," I said.

She just grabbed the menu from my hand and went into splits. She split herself, and on my mother's life I couldn't see the joke, so I said I wasn't hungry, but to tell you the truth my stomach was growling like a waterfall.

I sat and watched as she swallowed all the spaghetti and stuff. She kept saying I ought to try some, but I wasn't going to show myself up. If I'd said one thing, then I was going to stick to it. "I'm not hungry," I said.

When I left her at the bus-stop she asked me if I'd enjoyed my dinner. Real flippin' cheeky she was.

"Best portion of plaice and chips I've had in years, really crisp," I said, just to show I didn't have any hard feelings, even though my feelings were harder than exams. I'd paid for the dinner. I'd insisted.

"I've always enjoyed free dinners," she said, as she got on the 133 to Brixton from the Elephant. That's the kind of brass you don't need to polish, I thought, as I walked back home with my hands in my pockets.

I rang up Tony and told him it didn't work out. I tried to take Wendy out again, but she was going with this geezer from Scotland Yard who had a blue Cortina and she told me she didn't want to go out with schoolboys. I'd have asked Lorraine out again, but I felt she was only tolerating me and she didn't fancy me one bit. I thought about her a lot. She was a funny girl. I didn't speak to her in school after that evening. I don't know what it was, I can't quite put my finger on it, but I felt she was telling me somehow to keep my distance. When I was going with Wendy, I always got the feeling that she'd do her nut if I packed her in, but with Lorraine it was like she expected nothing, wanted nothing, she'd take what came, and wait for more to come.

Then she started taking the mick. It was in a General Studies class in the sixth form, and this teacher was going on about why the Irish were thick or something. He was saying that everybody thought that everybody else was thick, that it was natural, and if the British thought the Irish were not so smart, then the Jews thought the British were not so smart and the Americans thought that the British were all snobs or all Cockneys talked in rhyming slang and the like. Then Lorraine started shooting her mouth. There was only twelve of us in that class and we sat around a table in the sixth-form suite and this geezer never stopped talking about politics and racial relations and prejudice and all that crap. Lorraine always talked to him like she was the only one in the class and we was out in the playground playing marbles and she was on telly.

"That's what all white people think," she said. "It's just stupidness. They think Pakis are all Oxfam and niggers live in trees, and Chinese food is ying yang food."

I knew she was getting at me. Then the geezer asked us for our views, so I said, "I reckon that a lot of it is true, that blacks do live off Social Security, because there's a black feller on our estate and he drives a Benz, and polishes it up every Saturday and when you see him he's always got a new suit and he goes with white slags, a new one every two hours, and he never works. It's nothing to do with prejudice, it's just that a lot of white people pay a lot of tax and rates and that the blacks come in and take Social Security . . ."

"And eat a lot of free dinners," Lorraine said.

She was a bitch. She never talked to me after that. Not till we left school.

I'd meet someone from school down the Walworth Road and they'd say, "Watcha, Pete," and we'd have a talk. I wanted to be an architect, but I had to get my City and Guilds Draughtsman's exams first, so I was working with this firm on an apprenticeship. We'd talk about this and that and how much lolly we was taking home and about the old teachers and the old times. All the white kids I met from school knew that Wendy had gone for an Old Bill, and she was saying "hello, hello, hello" instead of "watcha". We didn't talk about the black kids, except for Keith, who wasn't like the rest of them and was trying to be a draughtsman himself. If I saw any of the blacks I'd been in school with, they would raise their hands, or just blank me, and we'd pass without a word. I thought a bit about Lorraine. If I met her again, I told myself, I'd ask her out, show her that I'd learnt a thing or two, I'd planned it all out in my head. We'd go to the same cinema and see some posh movie or other, whatever was running, and then I'd take her to a Chinese and order a Won-ton Soup and Crab in Ginger, Char Si Pong, the lot, just to show her that old Pete had learnt a thing or two with the lads at the firm who were fond of a curry or of a Chinese or pizza after a hard Friday night's drinking down the local. The lads would talk about a

Vindaloo and a Madras as though they was bloody veterans of the Burmese campaign.

When I actually met her, there was no chance. Well, I didn't exactly meet her. I just saw her and we exchanged a few words. It was like this. I was round Kilburn way, 'cos our office has a branch up there, and I was told to go and discuss some designs with a top geezer in our firm who worked in Kilburn. The lads from the Kilburn office sussed me out and, after, we went for a drink in a pub round their way. I didn't know them much, but I strung along.

The pub was a young scene, Friday night boppers from round the top end of the Edgware Road. There were lights popping all over the ceiling and huge mirrors on the walls which were otherwise plastered with old newspapers to give the place the look of being in the know. Up the end of the bar was this geezer doing the disco, leaning over his tube microphone and running down the soul.

"We're gonna have some dancing in a piece, Pete," Sol told me. "This is a nice scene, topless go-go, strippers, a pint of real ale, a real good time."

So the spotlight came on the stage and the disco geezer introduced the dancer. We were at the bar. A few of the lads had grabbed stools and I was standing with my pint with my back to the stage and the dance floor. When the music stopped I looked around. You could have knocked me down with a feather. Just outside the circle of the spotlight, like a ghost, like a bloody shivering ghost, stood Lorraine, in a dressing-gown which she was urging off her shoulders. Some black guy was waiting at the corner of the stage to catch it as it dropped. As the DJ finished his introduction, she strolled into the light in heels and gold knickers with purple tassles dangling from them and no bra. The pub had turned its attention to her, though I could see that the fellers in my mob were pretending to take it cool.

They were all screwing her and giving off that they weren't interested at all.

The strobe came on and the green and blue lights began flashing. Lorraine with her haunted face and wiry body began her dance, her skinny pair of legs like those of a delicate race-horse, slim, with the muscles running on the bone, shifting with some hesitance.

"I heard it through the grapevine, no longer will you be mine," sang Marvin Gaye, and the mob I was with began to hoot and clap.

"Look at the fucking state of it," said Sol. "Blimey, I'd rather go to Madame Tussaud's and see the Chamber of Horrors."

In the dark she couldn't see us, she couldn't have known where the voices were coming from. Between the stage and us there were these pillars, and I felt like disappearing behind one of them. She was dancing good, mind you, but it was true that she didn't have much meat on her.

She was a mover, give her that. And she had some guts, getting up in front of that mob and doing her thing.

"Oxfam," one of the lads shouted, and the faces in the darkness tittered.

"Spare ribs," Sol shouted, as she danced on.

"Knock it off," I said. "Don't show us up."

"Spare ribs," someone else shouted from the far end of the pub. She had small breasts, flat on her sinewy body. Of course she heard the voices, heard the laughter, but her expression didn't change. She was dancing for all she was worth, and her body moved gracefully through the tune, but there was no sex in it, if you know what I mean. She wasn't no topless dancer, and if she didn't realize it, the governor of the pub should've.

"Spare ribs." They'd picked it up at the other end of the

pub and were trying to give her the slow hand-clap. They were going at it like it was the first laugh they'd had that week.

The record finished and Lorraine stepped hastily out of the spotlight. The DJ quickly flipped turntables and started some soul sounds. I watched her as her man gave her the dressing-gown and she rushed into the ladies.

"The gaffer's not going to have her again," the barman said.

I left my pint on the bar and waited till she came out of the ladies. She was wearing a trouser suit and a band around her forehead. As I approached her I could see her mascara was smudged and she looked like she'd rather be on the Flying Scotsman to hell than right there in that pub. She was in a hurry, but she saw me and recognized me.

"Hello, Lorraine," I said, not knowing what else to say. I felt the lads had treated her something rotten, something shameful, and on my life if I'd been able to, I would have got them publicly on their knees to her.

She was as surprised as I was.

"I didn't know you hung around my ex-beat," she said.

"I didn't know you'd started professional dancing," I said.

"Well, you heard what the customers thought," she said.

"They're a load of stupid fuckers," I said. "Excuse the language. How're you getting on?"

I wanted to ask her for a drink, but it was the wrong place, the wrong moment. I wanted to tell her that I'd often thought of her, that now more than ever I wondered where she'd got to, what she was doing, how she kept herself. Her man come up and touched her elbow.

"I'll see you, Pete," she said.

"Yeah." I said.

"I'm dancing in another pub," she said. "Half an hour. Rough stuff, this, earning your dinners," and she smiled and walked away. I went back to my pint.

The last time I saw her was very brief. I met her on the pavement in Soho. It was raining. I'd finished my time at the firm and I'd bought this car and dropped my mate and girl-friend off at Gerrard Street. I'd gone to park the car. I saw her coming from a few yards down. She was with an old bald geezer in a posh raincoat. She was hanging on to his arm, dressed to the hilt, made up like a wedding cake. She looked stoned, too, unsteady on her feet.

"I saw you first this time," she said.

She stopped in front of me and smiled, and her mouth opened but her eyes stayed distant, like I'd known them, like they were when she was thinking of other things when we'd been there, children in the first year of school. The old man stood a little way behind her and she behaved as though he wasn't there. She put her fingers on my tie, and said, "How are you, Pete?"

I stepped back a bit.

"I'm just going to see some friends," I said.

"Have you seen anyone from the old school?" she asked. "I haven't seen any of them bastards," she added, veering on her feet.

"No, no, I haven't," I said.

"Oh, hang on," she said. "I saw your girl-friend Wendy. You know what she said to me?"

"Yes, Wendy," I said. "She's in the police, isn't she?"

"She too damn feisty. She catch me on my business," Lorraine said, her accent suddenly becoming black.

"Oh, oh," I said. "You been nicking from Woolworth's again, Lorraine?"

I shuffled my feet. I could see it coming.

78

"You see this, Pete," Lorraine said, taking one step back and pointing with a flowing hand at the pavement. "This here is the street. Your Wendy don't want me to walk the street and she is a po-lis." She nodded. Now I could see that she was drunk, but her eyes which stared into mine looked sober as the rising sun. "She don't like me walk the street, our Wendy," she said.

"Yes," I said. "What do you expect from the Old Bill? She wasn't ever my girl, Lorraine!"

"You want to get out of the rain, Pete," she said. She began to walk past me dragging the old geezer after her.

"Pete," she said, and turned round as though she'd forgotten something. "Pete, I'll see yuh." She was facing me again and she turned to the old geezer who looked impatient to shove off. "It's Pete, my old school mate. Pete, this is Mr Smith who's just going to buy me a free dinner."

SALT ON A SNAKE'S TAIL

There was the short route home from school and the long route. Jolil took the long route because by the time he got out of school the other boys who lived in his building had gone home. Mr Morrisson had kept him behind in his office and shown him some books.

"We must do something about your English," Mr Morrisson had said. "Come up to my room at ten to four and we'll go over some things together."

Jolil didn't want to refuse. He didn't want to tell Mr Morrisson why he was impatient to get home. He usually left the school gate with five or six of the other Asian boys. It wasn't planned, but it was necessary. If they walked home together, they could pass the gangs of older white boys who gathered outside the school gates without fear. They'd take the short route home, and if they passed the cluster of hostile faces outside the white estate at the end of their street, they could quicken their steps and feel the safe warmth of being part of a crowd. If you walked past there alone, you walked along the Whitechapel Road and came round to the flats the long way.

"I got something out of the public library specially for you, Jolil," Mr Morrisson said, and he handed Jolil a book on the martial arts. He had told Mr Morrisson some days before that that was what he was interested in.

"Don't just stare at the pictures, try and read some of it," Mr Morrisson said.

His father saw him clutching the thick book when he got home. "Go wash your face and say your prayers," Mr Miah said.

"We're not going to the mosque till later," Jolil protested. He headed for the inside room where he and his sisters slept. His father was already wearing his white muslin prayer cap. A bad sign, Jolil thought. It meant that his dad was in a lecturing mood. He would carry on at him.

"Get down to *namaaz*," he said sternly. "The devout must pray as many times on Friday as they can. There is no help for us but Allah. Who did you come home with?"

Jolil didn't reply. He sat on his bed and opened the book that Mr Morrisson had given him. Normally when he got home, his father would be working at the machines in the front room, sewing acres of cloth together, fulfilling the "contract". But Friday was the sabbath. The machines would stop. The women would be in the kitchen, his mother and sister-in-law. His father would prowl about the front room and give directives which most of them ignored.

Jolil had let Mr Morrisson into the secret. He had told him why he liked Kung Fu and Bruce Lee.

"Read anything, read comics if you must," Mr Morrison said. He didn't really catch on, Jolil thought, it was another reading exercise to him. His friend Errol knew about Kung Fu; he'd take him the book when he went over to his place on Saturday.

Jolil turned the pages. Bruce Lee's muscles almost bulged out of the photographs. His hands, fingers outstretched, seemed to be clawing magical strength out of the very air. The red scars on his body were supposed to be blood wounds, but they looked deliberately cut in neat patterns. And his face, Jolil thought, his face had the authoritative power of a humble man. Jolil tried to read the writing on the opposite page. He could read each word, but the sentences didn't seem to add up. The pictures couldn't actually tell you how to put the thing into practice, but they told a story all right. Bruce Lee was a simple man, probably a poor man when he started out. He even wore the clothes of an urchin, two sizes too small for a grown man. In one picture, he was in the air, a fierce animal, falling with puma-like fists on four shocked opponents.

Jolil rose from the bed and went to the mantelshelf and looked in the mirror. His mother came into the room and took the brass box of betel nut and cloth in which the betel leaves were wrapped.

"Go and wash your face, your father will be furious," she said. Jolil narrowed his eyes and undid three buttons on his shirt, staring into the mirror. He touched his cheek-bones. Yes, they were somewhat like Bruce Lee's.

"You bring this book of idols into the house?" his father suddenly asked. Jolil lowered his arms and turned round. His father had picked the book up off the bed and was leafing through it with an expression of severe disapproval. Mr Miah did a dry, coughing gargle in his throat, as though gathering his spit to show his contempt.

"It's from school," Jolil said.

"Who leads young men astray with all these pictures of half-naked actors?" Jolil's father asked. "Who is it that teaches young men this sort of disrespect?"

"Give it to me. I'll put it away," Jolil said, trying to take the book from his father's hands.

"You should be reading the Koran. I shall still be grateful to Allah, even though he's given me an infidel son. You'd better read the books that matter, son, before you take up all these Chinaman's tricks. You don't reply when your father asks you questions anymore, eh?"

"What questions?" Jolil asked, trying to distract his father's attention while he grabbed the book and looked around for a hiding place for it.

"Who did you come home from school with?"

"Errol."

"Errol, eh? Well, it's time you stopped running around with the darkies. You should be down in the basement learning to read Arabic with Kazi-sahab."

"All the babies go to Kazi's class," Jolil replied.

"You are never too old to humble yourself and learn the words of Allah."

"Anyway, I know Arabic. I know Urdu . . . aleph, be, pe, the, zaal, zin and everything."

"The only Urdu you know is from those rubbish films. You have no respect, bringing rubbish books into the house, and dirty pictures of actors and Chinamen."

"He's not an actor," Jolil said. "He's a tiger."

"A common wrestler. Tigers are stupid creatures anyway. They live outside the grace of God; they fall into pits built with twigs and leaves to trap them."

Jolil knew when his father was about to begin some story about Bangladesh. He'd heard this one twenty times, about the tiger who thought that every trodden path had been paved by his own paws and was surprised to find a monkey loping along the cleared track to his water-hole. Jolil didn't want to hear the end of it. He turned and went into the kitchen and asked his sister-in-law when his brother would be home.

"He's gone to the meeting."

"They always have these useless meetings. They are becoming Godless in this wretched country; they think they can fight white men. You know how many white men there are?" his father asked, walking into the kitchen. The women made no reply.

"I wanted to go to the meeting," Jolil said.

"They will talk. Bengalis love to talk big talk," his father said.

There had been an incident in the previous week. A Bengali had been stabbed in the ear on his way home from work. The white gang that stabbed him had run away. Some people in the flats where Jolil's family lived had called a meeting of all the families. His elder brother, Khalil, had gone and returned with the news that they were planning some defence of their buildings. The night of the stabbing, gangs of Bengali youths had set out from the cafés on Brick Lane, determined to challenge any white gang that offered insult or violence. Then the next day someone had thrown a brick through the window of the ground-floor flat and another meeting had been called, this time of the whole building.

"If they want a war, there's going to be a war," Khalil said when he returned.

"What can you do if God's will is not with you?"

"Leave God aside," Khalil replied. "We're going to store bricks and stones on the terrace, and if a gang turns up to attack, we can all go up there and deal with them."

"If a snake stings you once, you don't turn round and chase it so it can sting you again. Leave it alone," Mr Miah said to his eldest son.

"What do you do if it turns round to sting you again?"

"You put salt on its tail," Mr Miah said.

He always said that sort of thing as though it were God's truth. Sometimes Jolil wanted to argue with him. He couldn't make sense of his dad's proverbs. His dad would say, each grain of rice bears the name of the person who's destined to eat it. Or he'd say, you put salt on a snake's tail and it'll never bother you again. Another day he'd shout at Jolil for spilling grains of salt on the kitchen floor while sprinkling his chips and tell him that when he appeared before God, he would be made to pick up every grain of salt he'd wasted in his lifetime with his eyelids before he'd be allowed past the gates of heaven. It was all nonsense.

But Mr Miah used a no-nonsense tone to say it in. They were the truths of life, just like going to the mosque on

Fridays, and working at the machine when your father told you to.

Jolil would only assist with the sewing work when a contract had to be urgently finished. He'd skip school and help his father and sister-in-law who sat all day at the two machines in their front room. When a contract was "urgent", the machines would spread their clatter into the night. Jolil didn't like machining, but he wouldn't tell his dad. Mr Miah said there were two types of money, sweat money and water money, and with water money you couldn't keep a family alive, you could only gamble it away or buy water with it. You had to sweat if you wanted to eat. Jolil would load the thread on to the machines, he'd wind up reels of nylon and separate sewn pieces from the piles of cut material every hour, he'd fetch the tea and he'd run down to the shop for condensed milk and cigarettes when he was asked to.

"You'll have to miss school on Monday and work at these linings," his father said.

"Why can't we finish it over the week-end?"

"We don't work on the sabbath," Mr Miah said, "and on Sunday we're going to Dog Market to get some chairs. We have to get your mother some chairs."

"I have to go to school on Monday."

"What for? Since when have you become so fond of learning?"

"They're going to show a Kung Fu film to all the third years."

"They waste your time in school," his father said. "What use is that to you in becoming a tailor?"

"It's not an ordinary film," Jolil said. "It's about the secrets of Kung Fu. Mr Morrisson is bringing a film which will explain everything."

"Everything can never be explained," his father said. "If

88

you carry on in this useless way, I'll send you back to Bangladesh and you can learn to be a begging wrestler, go from village to village and challenge all the idiots to fight."

"I'll work tomorrow. I can do a hundred linings in a day," Jolil said.

He'd do it, he thought. When they'd been at the old house, there was still some joy left in this business, making the needle hum between your fingers. Tailoring made nimble but tired fingers. It turned your fingers into tools. Kung Fu converted them into weapons.

These were thoughts his father wouldn't understand. In a movie called *The Black Dragon Revenges the Death of Bruce Lee*, the hero had plucked out the eyes of several villains and destroyed with similar cruelty the faces of others. There was a knack to it. You twisted your palm in the faces of the enemy. Your hurricane hands had to be trained to lay low an army of fiends. Once he was good enough, Jolil told himself, he'd allow people to photograph him. That's the kind of hero he wanted to be. Once he was good enough he'd get his photograph in the *Martial Arts* magazine, and in *Filmfare*, which his sister-in-law read. He'd be the first Bangladeshi martial arts hero, and his films would sell better than those of Rajesh Khanna, whom his sister-in-law adored, and then he could buy a big white American car. But if he ever became famous, he wouldn't go and live in Malabar Hill in Bombay like the other film stars did. He'd use his powers to do other things, to right a lot of wrongs, to be a saint of the fighting world.

His father had once told Jolil a story about a wise man being reborn in a remote village in Sylhet. He said the souls of old bandits implanted themselves in the bodies of new-born babies and returned as flesh in the families of saintly people. Wisdom passes from man to man, his father said. Strength is God-given and can't be extinguished; it's like a flame which leaves not only embers but heat behind it. And Jolil wondered whether the soul of Bruce Lee would pass into the body of an up-and-coming young hero. It was one of his father's stories that he wanted to believe.

In the past few months, Mr Miah had come up with a lot of these stories. Jolil had noticed that the more trouble there was, the more philosophical his father became. He would put on his prayer-cap and he would mutter at the rest of the family. Khalil had stopped paying any attention to him.

Khalil said there'd be more trouble. When the summer came the whites would go on the rampage, they'd maybe come with guns. Khalil's mates all said that they wanted to be ready, but Jolil knew that they didn't know how to be ready for them. The first task was to protect their building. There were fifty Bengali families there. They were all squatters. They had moved into the building amid tremendous excitement. Some young Bengalis had moved the first family in, and the news had spread through Brick Lane and its environs. Like the rest, Jolil's family had quit their little back room in their relatives' house and moved their mattresses and utensils to the new place. It wasn't new at all, of course. It was an old building that nobody else wanted. On the first day there had been a lot of coming and going. The police came and white men from the government came in vans and spoke to the two or three young men who were conducting the whole operation. They had settled in and a month later the trouble began. Some of the Bengalis were very fierce. They'd make tough speeches about fighting and about protecting their families and their own people. Jolil's father didn't make any speeches, at least not in public. He argued with Khalil at home.

Khalil would say, "This is a *jehad*, a holy war. If we want to stay in this country, we have to fight."

And yet Khalil brushed his hair to look like a film star and put on his best clothes and went out with his friends, strolling up and down Whitechapel Road and Brick Lane and making trips to the West End. Even Khalil didn't understand what it was they had to do. Strolling around Brick Lane wouldn't make you strong, wouldn't build you up and strike terror in the guts of the "rubbish" whites. Jolil was determined to practise the arts of discipline and meditation, because Mr Morrisson had told him that being an expert at anything was difficult. At the root of all strength was discipline and meditation. But how was it to be done? He'd hit the palm of his hand against the wall a hundred times and count to a hundred because the counting kept his mind off the pain.

When he was indoors, or outside in the courtyard with the younger children from their building, he'd practise his kicks. He'd try and raise his knee higher each time, flicking his foot out from under, imitating lightning. He still struggled to retain his balance. One day he'd be perfect. He'd go to Kung Fu classes and win himself a black belt.

Jolil knew that Errol was also training. And Errol had learnt modesty. He'd never show off in the playground at school. He wouldn't raise a fist or a leg. But Jolil knew that Errol had hardened his palms with careful persistence and he could break planks of wood at a stroke if he wanted. He showed Jolil how to twist his fist when he pushed it out to arm's length. That was one of the secrets. It was a controlled, graceful movement and you had to learn to get it just right. And fast. Speed was another secret. Silence was yet another. Strength was more terrifying if it wasn't expected. You had to look like a priest and fight like a tiger. Then there was confidence. One of the reasons Jolil didn't practise his strokes in front of Errol or any of the other boys in school, was that they might laugh at him. When they laughed, your spirit got soaked up, and then no matter how fast and rough your fists were, you'd be defeated by their stares and their grins. Your confidence had to defeat those stares and grins.

"Put your cap on, we're going to prayers now," Mr Miah said. Jolil got his jacket on and put his prayer-cap in his pocket. He wasn't going into the street with it on. His father strode slightly ahead of him. It was still light when they came out of the flats and passed under the old archway. His father turned left. They were going to take the route past the white estate. The younger children were still playing in the courtyard. They wandered around the piles of debris and stalked through the deserted basements, climbing in and out through window sills with their frames ripped out. Their voices, a mixture of Bengali and sharp English exclamations, echoed round the yard. The sound of sewing machines and the odour of frying spices floated out of open doorways.

"You hear them?" Jolil's father said. "They won't stop their machines for judgement day. They shouldn't call themselves Muslims. See what the promise of a few pence does to our people?"

He gathered his spit and fired it out of his mouth on to the pavement. They walked across the narrow cobbled street, past the boarded-up warehouses towards the mosque. Jolil knew that the kids from the white estate at the end of that street called this territory "Paki-land". They'd have to pass through those shabby concrete flats and then they'd be safe again. The new concrete would give way again to the half-gutted complex of old factories and houses, the smell of "pig-lard" as his father called it in Bengali, would give way again to the richer scents of garlic and coriander from the warren of Asian dwellings which surrounded the territory of the mosque.

Jolil saw them, and saw that his father had spotted them too: a group of about a dozen white boys and girls, leaning against and sitting on the concrete parapets that surrounded their estate. They should have gone the other way round, Jolil thought. He took a couple of hurried steps to walk abreast of his father. His father's steps became shorter and faster. He was staring straight into space, as though he was unaware of the eyes of the crowd that greeted their approach. A small lump came into Jolil's throat. It wasn't too late to turn round and go the other way, even if it meant an extra half-mile to walk. But that was what they mustn't do. His father walked on as though the thought hadn't occurred to him.

As they approached, the gang stopped their chatter. They stood sultry and silent. Jolil looked at their feet as he passed, he didn't want to look up in their faces in case they took that as a provocation. They looked massive, these white youths, in their close-fitting clothes and their close-cropped hair.

"Allah will guide us," Jolil's father muttered, as though to himself.

They walked past the gang and a voice called out from behind them, "Oi, Pak-a-mac."

"Keep walking," Jolil's father said to him, pretending to be in charge of their pace which was light with the lift of fear. Jolil could see that his father was afraid. Maybe even this gang of louts could smell the stink of funk that came off him.

"Can't wait now, eh?" one of the boys said. "Got to rush off and put in some overtime." He was trying to imitate an Asian accent.

"Leave off, Baz," one of the girls on the parapet said. "One of these days these blokes are going to lay a hiding on you."

93

"Don't make me laugh," the boy said. "The only hiding these geezers know is under their beds when there's trouble. Even that won't help them soon, though."

Mr Miah's step had broken into a kind of run.

"You'll have to run all the way back to the jungle," a voice from the mob shouted behind them.

"You see why the Koran forbids us to drink?" asked Jolil's father. Jolil didn't reply.

At the mosque Jolil tried to concentrate on his prayers. His heart was still beating fast. What could they have done, he was thinking. He looked round at the other men who were on their knees, bending their bodies to the intonation of the prayers. Jolil felt a sense of calm. All these people, he thought, all these people. They can't drive us anywhere. Khalil had said that the whites wanted to drive them back by scaring them, making them so afraid to walk the streets that they'd have to pack up and go back to Bangladesh.

He looked up at his father. His panic seemed to have passed away and he looked serenely absorbed in his prayers, opening and closing his eyes. A little threat, a little discomfort, that was what life offered you, he seemed to be thinking. Jolil knew his father. To him it wasn't important. Maybe it wasn't important to all this crowd on their knees. Like the snow and the early dark in winter, this threat and hatred that had been loosed all round their surrounded lives, was just part of the fact of England. Like the kites in the skies over the villages in Bangladesh, or the locusts that swept the crops, coming like the monsoon in fatal clouds, these "rubbish whites" as they called them, were creatures with whom one had to share the landscape. For Jolil they were different. For six years he'd been to school with white kids. He knew every twist of the language they spoke. He understood the jokes they made. He knew their reasons and their unreason. To his father they were people to be ignored, their remarks were like the noise of crows in the trees towards sunset; they signified nothing.

After coming out of the mosque, Jolil noticed that his father lingered around until they were joined in the street by other men from their building.

"Never be scared of jackals," he said to Jolil. "If those white men had tried to attack us or anything I would have taught them a good lesson."

"We should go round the other way," Jolil said.

"Oh no," his father replied. "Streets were made to walk on." And he spat with conviction.

"You should have spat at them when they abused us," Jolil said.

"My mouth was dry, boy."

The next afternoon Jolil was at Errol's place. Errol's room was plastered with Kung Fu posters. Jolil told Errol about the book that Mr Morrisson had given him.

"Some high books on Kung Fu, boy, only black belts could understand them. It ain't like foo'ball where anyone can see the tricks. Kung Fu is a heavy science, boy; if you don't know the meditation, then you can't do nothing," Errol said.

They discussed the film they were going to see. Morrisson had told them that it was called *The Secrets of Kung Fu*. Errol said maybe the film could teach him a couple of things, there were still one or two things he needed to know.

When Jolil got home his father and sister-in-law were at the machines. His father would normally give up his seat to Jolil and go off to the mosque on his own, leaving Jolil to work for a couple of hours. This day he didn't budge. He turned to his daughter-in-law and said she could have a rest now that Jolil had returned. They worked in silence. His father hadn't told the others at home about the incident the previous evening.

On Sunday Jolil set out with his father to Dog Market. It was crowded. People walked between rows of junk shops on either side. The stalls sold everything from vegetables to antique gramophones. His father poked his head into several second-hand shops and looked around for a set of chairs.

"Wanting chair, good chair," he said to the man with the huge belly who sat outside one of the shops.

"What sort of chairs?"

"For sitting down."

"Look in there, mate, I've got plenty of chairs."

"How much price?"

His father walked to the back of the shop which was piled with mattresses and old tables and canvas sheets and broken furniture. He lifted a well-polished chair off the top of the pile.

"Those are no good to you, mate," the man said. "They're antiques."

"How much?" his father insisted.

"What's the point of telling you if you ain't gonna want them?"

"I want them," Mr Miah said. Jolil could see that his father understood that this shopkeeper was trying to insult him.

"All right, let's say twelve pound each, all right? Satisfied?"

Mr Miah put the chair back on top of the pile.

"Come and have a dekko at these, mate, more your sort of thing. Good strong chairs, these, last till your boy has grandchildren running all over Spitalfields. They're two quid each," the man added, handing the steel-framed, plastic-covered chairs to Mr Miah. He dusted the chairs off.

Mr Miah handed over the money.

"I know your people, mate. I know what they like," the man said.

Jolil took one chair and his father took the other. They passed through the crowd.

"You've got to know how to get things at their proper price – these traders are very sharp," his father said to Jolil as they emerged from the bustle of the market. Jolil knew they'd been insulted, the man had jeered at them. He walked with his eyes on the pavement. There was no way a man could swallow an insult and still look the world in the eye. One day, he thought, one day he'd be ready. He wouldn't accept walking in fear.

As they turned down Chicksand Street, on the last lap home, pausing every few yards and transferring the awkward weight of the chairs from arm to arm, Jolil saw two of the youths who had been in the gang on Friday night. They were standing on the pavement, leaning against the wall as they had done that night.

"These rubbish people are still there," his father said. "When they are in ones and twos they are not so bold, eh? I'll smash this chair over their heads if they say anything to me." He was strolling with confidence now.

"Men should be as afraid of killing as they are of dying," he said, and gathering his spit, he spat on the pavement.

"What are you spittin' outside our flats for?" one of the white boys said as they approached them.

"Leave it, leave it, leave it," Mr Miah said in English.

"I'll give you leave it," one of the boys said, stepping forward as they passed him.

"Just keep walking, just hold the chair out if he comes," Mr Miah said in Bengali to Jolil.

The youth was upon them. He grabbed Mr Miah's jacket

collar from the back. He tried to wrench loose, dropping his chair. The boy wore a red sweater, and its tightness made his muscles look menacingly large. There was a flash of spite in his face.

"Oi, you want to go and clean up that gob you made there."

"No, thank you," said Jolil's father, hastily. "Just move on, hurry on," he added, in Bengali, to Jolil.

"Ah, no-speak-d-English, eh? You know damn well what I said, now come back here and clean it up."

The other youth came strolling up and positioned himself in front of Jolil's father.

"You ain't bolting anywhere, curly-caps," he said. "You're going to do as my mate says and clean up your gob."

He picked up the chair that Mr Miah had dropped and banged it emphatically on the pavement. Then he sat on it.

"Why you trouble an old man?" Jolil's father said. He was beginning to plead. Suddenly Jolil felt he couldn't take it any more. "Get off, it's our chair," he said, rushing up to the seated youth and trying to pull the chair from under him.

"You want to digest your teeth, Paki junior?" the youth said.

"It's a very young boy, little boy," his father said, holding up his hand as if in surrender. He walked back to the place where he'd spat and began shuffling his shoes over the pavement.

"I said with your tongue, not with your Tesco bombers," the young man said.

Jolil picked up the chair he'd been carrying, lifted it and rushed at the young man. He nimbly stepped aside, jerked the chair out of Jolil's hands and flung it a few yards off. Then he jumped on Jolil and slapped him with his open hands on both cheeks, pushing him off as Jolil rushed at him in between the resounding flat blows.

"Don't you get funny with me," the youth said between his teeth. Jolil threw himself at him again. The youth got him by the front of his shirt, held him at arms' length and flung him to the ground. Then he pounced on him, kicking him, as Jolil tried to cover his face.

Then he heard his father's voice behind the young man.

"Very sorry, very sorry," he was saying, and then in Urdu, "in the name of all-seeing Allah."

The youth who was kicking Jolil let out a little yelp.

"Aaaaah, you bastard," Jolil heard him say, and he fell to his knees as though he had dropped something on the pavement. Jolil's father screamed to him to run, to leave the chairs. He scrambled to his feet and ran after his father. For a few seconds the other youth ran behind them and then he turned and went back to his companion who was still kneeling on the pavement, screaming as though he had looked in the face of murder. Jolil didn't turn. Neither he nor his father stopped till they reached the broken archway of their own building.

Khalil was at home when they walked in.

"What about the chairs?" his mother asked, and then, seeing the red marks on Jolil's face, "Oh, my God, what's happened to you?"

"We couldn't find any chairs," his father said. "Jolil tripped and fell down as we were coming back."

"I didn't," Jolil shouted. "We ran . . ." he started to say.

"Don't call your father a liar," Mr Miah said. "Go inside and wash your face."

"Why did you run away?" Khalil demanded. "Who chased you? I'll kill them."

"I'm not a man of violence," his father said, "and the day that sons of mine can tell their father what to do, is the day I want to stop living."

"If you live like a rat you've already stopped living," Khalil said.

"Don't answer back, boy. Nobody's been hurt. We're all right. Allah has brought us safely home."

Khalil wasn't going to speak against Allah. He turned on his heel and walked out of the house.

Jolil's face was burning now, with the slap and with the shame he felt. He didn't venture to tell his mother what had happened. He felt they had lost more than the chairs; they had lost the right to walk on the street. They had lost face. His feet, which should have been shooting kicks at the jaws of danger, had followed each other hastily home.

That night he lay on his back awake, his mind filled with the rage of their helplessness. The house was dark, the rest of the family was asleep. Jolil heard a noise in the kitchen. He heard the tap running and the sound of feet trying to tiptoe and then the sound of creaking wood. He got up from his bed and went through the front room quietly and peered into the kitchen. His father was kneeling on the floor in the dark. He turned his head over his shoulder, startled at Jolil's approach.

"Go back to sleep," he said, sternly.

Jolil stood in the darkened doorway, not obeying his father. The dirty lino on the floor of the kitchen had been turned up, and his father was fiddling with a hammer with one of the floorboards. "Listen, son," he said, getting to his feet and turning round, whispering almost. "Don't ever tell anyone, not even your mother or Khalil, that we bought any chairs or about those men."

"I won't," Jolil said. They had run away; he didn't want to tell anyone that his father was a coward. "Don't worry. I won't."

The next morning his mother brought some white paste

she'd made up and put it on Jolil's cheek. Jolil washed it off, brushed his hair, and, taking the long route, went to school.

In the darkness of the sports' hall, the kids whistled and cheered as Bruce Lee appeared on the screen, leaping over walls, dodging out of the path of bullets, tackling six of his enemies at the same time and laying them flat. Then the film turned from colour to black-and-white. A man in a suit was addressing the audience. ". . . so we take a look at the world in which the stars of this international cult live. We look at the way in which this game is played, we look at the magic and illusion of Kung Fu . . ." There were more shots of men lopping off other men's heads with the swipe of a braced palm. The blood flowed and the third year cheered. Then the white man came on the screen again. He was going to explain, Jolil thought, he was going to give away the secret. As he talked, the picture showed the crew of a film studio setting things up in the background. Then the Chinese man, to whom the white man had been talking, jumped off a wall on which he was perched. The cameramen recorded the jump. The man threw his arms out as he leapt. The white commentator held the film up to the audience.

"So we play it backwards," he said. The film inside the film was played backwards and it showed the same jump in reverse, looking like the Chinese man had jumped up on to the wall.

Jolil watched it in silence. The film moved to other rooms in the studio. An actor posed next to a dummy of himself.

"Ain't it good," one of the boys next to him said.

The dummy's head was struck off, the fountains of blood began to pour from it, and its neck was held up to the camera to show how the blood was made to gush out of a pen-sized capsule. "All this happens at twenty-four frames a second in an ordinary film, the speed of normal life. What happens when you slow the camera down?" There was another shot of the Chinese man aiming kicks to the jaws of other actors. He did it slowly, deliberately, and the director of the film posed the extras in expressions of surprise. There was another shot of the same action at what seemed to be incredible speed.

"Celluloid has created the Kung Fu superman, running, leaping and fighting with fists of speeded-up fury."

The whole film was like that. When the lights were switched on and Mr Morrisson came to the front of the hall and said that they'd have ten minutes extra on their lunchtime, Jolil turned to Errol. Most of the others were indifferent to what they had seen.

"In the book that Morrisson gave me, it said that Bruce Lee could really jump on to a ten-foot wall."

"Bruce Lee dead," Errol replied.

"It's stupid, I reckon," said another boy in their row. "Kung Fu is for mongs."

"White man spoil everything," Errol said.

Jolil didn't stay to school in the afternoon. He went back home. He couldn't make up his mind about how he felt about the shattered secret. Maybe the film was lying, all Kung Fu was not like that, it wasn't all tricks.

When he got to their building, Jolil could see three police cars parked outside. There were policemen in the courtyard and several people from the flats were outside talking to them. The women and children leaned out of the windows.

Jolil burst through the door of their flat. His father was sitting at the machine, his spectacles sliding down his nose.

"What's going on here? What're the police doing in our buildings?"

"You want to mind the world's business? You'll have to

have a million lives."

"A white boy was stabbed at the end of the street yesterday evening," Khalil said. Khalil was looking out of their window. "The police want to know if any of the children found a knife or anything in the street while playing."

"Why should we get involved in white man's quarrels?" his father said, threading the machine after licking the thread.

"It wasn't a white man who stabbed him," Khalil said. "It was some Bengalis and they left some chairs behind on the pavement."

"Don't talk loosely, letting your tongue wag in your head. We've got all the chairs we need in this house," his father said, still at the machine.

Then he turned to Jolil. "Go and take two pounds from my purse and go down to Brick Lane and buy me a pair of cutters' scissors. Take the long route."

GO PLAY BUTTERFLY

"I 'll fix you to fly away," the young man said. Then he asked Esther to hold still while he pinned on her wings. It was two nights before the Carnival, and Esther was aglow with the importance of it.

She hadn't wanted to do it at first. She didn't even know what Carnival was, but her mother had decided for her. Josephine, her friend from school, and Carol, who lived down the road, were both Trinidadians, and their mums had decided that they would "play" with a band. Carol had boasted about her costume in the presence of Esther's mum. It was too much of a challenge. Esther knew that her mother would pick up the gauntlet and that she would be made to "play mas" too.

Carol's family were moving. Her mother, who came and gossiped with Esther's mother, told endless stories about the beauty of their new house in Norwood. Everything she said implied that they'd finished with Brixton, finished with living in a council flat. They were home owners now. There were to be lace curtains and a new colour telly and a fence which was to be painted pink, and a bedroom for Carol and one for Stanley and one for the twins, and a dining-room which was separate from the kitchen. It was too much for Esther's mother, Mistress Waters, to take. And now Carol was in a band which was going to have its photograph in the *South London Press*, her mum said.

When Manny came home, Mistress Waters questioned him closely. What was all this Carnival business? Couldn't Esther take part in it if they wanted her to? Manny said he knew Soaky who was the artistic director of one of the "mas camps"; he could get her in, even at this late date, no problem. Manny was Esther's stepfather. She liked him. He knew everyone. He took her to the mas camp the next day. Esther could see that at first he wasn't too taken by the idea, but her mum had said it must be so, and it was.

The camp was a huge disused factory in Paddington. Manny drove Esther there and left her with his friend Soaky, a man with greying temples and a long straight nose, strange on the face of a black man. Esther was uncomfortable. Soaky's real name was Mr Dix, but all the kids in the camp called him Soaky. So Esther called him Soaky too. As soon as they walked in through the factory doors, a little gate, hinged into a larger one, Esther began to feel that sense of wanting to be anywhere but there. It was a place which would challenge her. It was a hive of activity. There were young men and women, most of them much older than Esther, working away at the trestles and the nylon and the tinsel, at tables all over the large and disorderly room. They didn't look up from their work when she came in with Manny, who sought Soaky out and introduced his daughter.

Soon, Manny became enthusiastic about the mas camp. He liked to take the drive to Paddington, and would volunteer to take Esther there. He began speaking about the camp as though it was his own enterprise. Esther knew that he was eager to carry her because it enabled him to get away from her mother. He would plant her in the camp and go off for a few hours, making his rounds in "the Grove", and hanging around the betting shops of Notting Hill. He would come back to pick her up, elevated or exhausted with the tensions of placing money on a horse.

On their second visit to the camp, Soaky had asked Esther to help make the costumes. He called out to a group of youths who were busy painting the stretched fabric of the dresses that the players would wear. Their band was called "Fantasia of the Ethereal Air". Soaky took Esther round to the youths and said, "Give this girl some wings; she go play butterfly."

The young men, four of them, were sizing Esther up. One of them was called Jojo, and he smiled at her. Another of them said they were going to make her "high, high" and asked her if a man had ever made her feel so light and airborne before. Esther was only fourteen. Men didn't speak to her like that. At least, she hadn't known them to before then. She kissed her teeth and turned her head away, pretending to look at the group of girls who were kneeling round another masquerader, pinning a costume on her with safety pins and needles clasped in their teeth. Esther moved away from Jojo and Claude and the rest of them and joined the group of women who were dyeing feathers.

From the day she had come there she had sensed that they had all treated her like she had never been treated before. Jojo and his mob had made remarks about her size. Manny had told Soaky that she was only fourteen, and the boys had said that she was "fit" and Manny had looked at them as though to say they'd gone too far. That's what they made her feel, Esther thought, older than herself. It was the first time that she'd been made self-conscious by a group of boys about her body. It was not only the way they looked it up and down, not only the way their eyes seemed to say that she had some magnetism. It was also the first time that she was going to be one of the stars. And the other stars were women much older than herself, girls who swirled in and out of the camp and were attended with the respect due to beauty, to flourish, to independence. Esther was happy to be in that team, amongst the forty women who were to play mas with Fantasia.

Twice when Esther had been there, the star of their band had walked into the mas camp. Esther thought she was gorgeous. She had an imperial look; a black beauty with a touch of disdain on her face. Esther knew that she was called Veronica. Soaky spoke of her as his leading lady. She stood at the door like someone who owned the place but still wanted to be treated like a visiting queen. The camp gathered round her when she walked in and held out her arms to be measured finally for the draperies that were to envelop them. She held back her head when Soaky and an assistant lifted the head-dress, peacock feathers and nylon and gold and black antlers, like a crown.

Yes, she would be Carnival Queen. There couldn't be anyone in this town more regal, more befitting the honour than her, and yet Esther didn't want to pay her tribute. As she watched Jojo and his cronies, Esther saw that they didn't want to pay her tribute either. The four young men carried on with their painting and pinning as though Veronica were a passing show in which they weren't interested, while Soaky and the other designers fawned around her, adjusting this and bringing up that, layer upon layer of costume, which, when it was assembled, looked light and natural on her lithe brown body.

Now there were two reasons why Esther wanted to be in this Carnival business. There was Veronica, who was to Esther an immediate rival. Esther watched her. Ten years older, she estimated. Until a few months ago she couldn't tell anyone's age, but she knew this girl was twenty-four. She must grow up like that, Esther thought, and while doing it she must avoid some of the shortcomings of this person. Her eyebrows were shaved too thin, Esther noticed, much too thin to seem at all natural. And her voice. It was wrong. There was too much girlish excitement and high-pitchedness in it. When she was that age, her voice would have more command in it. And it would lose the suggestion of giggle which came through when Veronica pronounced herself delighted with the head-dress.

Veronica looked around and Esther saw her looking all the mas players up and down, as quickly and unnoticeably as she could. That was all right, Esther decided, standing on the periphery of the orbit of the queen. That was the way the sun should cast its light on the outer planets that turn a constant face or rotate in its light.

Then there was Jojo. There was something very deliberate about the way he wasn't impressed by the leading lady. He looked at Veronica as he would at any other brother or sister who came to put in a bit towards the task of getting their collective glory on the road. Not only that, he exchanged glances with Esther, and smiled at her. He was working on a hundred wings and she was as important to him as the woman who was undoubtedly going to be Carnival Queen.

Two nights before Carnival there was a party at the camp. Manny took Esther, after persuading Mistress Waters to let her go. After all, he said, she wasn't going to go to the big Carnival dance, so she should at least get a Coke and some crisps at the camp. Mistress Waters had agreed reluctantly. She set out the most childish-looking, high-collared blouse for Esther to wear. But Esther had made other plans. She had persuaded Manny to buy her a blouse with a plunging neckline which would allow the brown crescents of her breasts to show. When she dressed for the party, Esther took a white cardigan and put it on to hide her blouse from her mother. In the car, she took it off and threw it on the back seat and pulled some lipstick out of her bag. Manny looked at her while he was driving but didn't say anything.

There were plenty of girls at the party. Some of the younger ones began dancing in pairs and trios. They danced as they would at school. If Carol and Josie had been there, Esther thought, or Sharon, or Nancy, she would have danced too. But alone, she felt stiff and self-conscious.

Manny was in high spirits. He walked around the crowd with a can of Special Brew. At one end of the hall the steel band played. When it stopped, the reggae amplifiers were switched on. At the other end of the hall, Jojo and his friends were still working away, putting the last touches to

111

their artistry. Esther wandered over from the circle of revellers to the row of workers.

"You get away from your father?" Jojo asked, not looking up from his work.

"Mm, hmm," Esther replied, conscious that he was going to look up at her any moment, see her in her new blouse.

"You want to go rave in the blues, or you want help me a second?" Jojo asked.

"Depends," Esther said.

He looked up and smiled.

"I design a new wing-thing here. See this triple fold with a clip?"

"Very interesting," Esther said, mocking him.

"You want to wear it?"

"I'm all right."

"Look, it'll make you light, take the weight off your platform shoe there."

"I'm not heavy anyway."

"You go be an ariel creature," he responded, picking up the folds of cloth he had on the table before him. "Just try it on, nuh?"

The nylon stretched between her wrists and her hips, in a huge fan.

"Hold this end from here," he said, kneeling beside her to pin the flaps of nylon and twist them around the spar that held the wings together. His fingers curled gently round her wrist, a grip that seemed to take all the weight out of her forearm. She was alive to the brushing, firm touch. She felt the blood coming up to her shoulders, up the side of her ribs and down her spine as though it was coming up to her head and going down at the same time.

"I go pin your blouse from the back," he said. "I go put my hand under your skirt."

Esther wanted to shut her eyes, gently let the lids drop,

112

shut out the world and feel for the moment nothing but the tingle of his fingers, but she kept them wide open. The others were looking at her. They'd laugh at her.

"Mind the pin," she said.

"You scared of a little poke?"

The other young man, who was working on a head-dress, heard Jojo and he smirked.

"Get on with your business," Esther said, knowing she'd spoiled the moment.

Jojo was behind her, pulling the back of her blouse away from her skin to get his hand under it.

"How old are you?" he asked softly in her ear.

"I'm sixteen," Esther lied.

"You got short arms for sixteen."

"I'm a girl not a monkey."

"Manny told me you only fourteen. He want to warn me."

"Manny don't know anything, only my mother knows our ages."

"He knows the age of every horse on the course."

"My mum says he can remember their birthdays, but not his own children's."

"You going to the Carnival dance?"

"I don't know, I might have something better to do."

"No one have better to do on Carnival night. It's constant jamming in seventy-six."

"I'll see," Esther said, knowing that her mother had already told her she couldn't go to any dance, even though she and Manny were going.

"You too young, eh?"

"Look, this thing comes right to my fingers."

"Caterpillar have to get used to being a butterfly," Jojo said.

"You too cheeky."

"I like your cheeks too."

"Tcha, stop your nonsense, man," Esther said in her most grown-up voice. She was afraid now that the rest of them had seen them in some intimate talk, and she turned round to face him. His expression was sullen. She'd expected him to be smiling. He wasn't. He was flaring the nylon out with his hands and frowning with dissatisfaction at the effect.

"It'll need two inches off, both ends. I'll have to work tonight, all night."

"It'll take you half an hour."

"You know nothing, Cata," he said.

Esther hated the new nickname. His tone said that she had let him down. Not because her arms were not long enough, but somehow she didn't seem to fit his expectation of her. She hadn't fitted perfectly into his creation. Suddenly she had become to him a clothes dummy, stiff, an object to size up in inches. She saw him go back to the work bench and place the wings out flat on it and stare at them, thoughtfully. Esther noticed his long, thin fingers, the way they smoothed the nylon with pride in their handiwork.

Esther felt that she couldn't control all the thoughts and feelings that ran chaotically through her at that moment. His hands had radiated their warmth, even though they hadn't touched her stockinged thighs. When she had cast her glance down towards him, his eyes had seemed to say, "Don't be scared, don't dig nothing, this ain't a skank, this is business." It was only when she was back in her bed at home, trying to recall the sensation of the brush of his wrist against her hip-bone, that she decided that the look in his eyes meant something more. It said, "This ain't a skank, this is business," but it also said that if she wanted to forget the business, there was a skank awaiting her.

On the night of the Carnival dance, Mistress Waters put Esther to bed and went out with Manny. Esther stayed awake. The next day, the next morning, she'd be out playing mas. She couldn't sleep, she was restless. She heard Manny and her mum return in the early hours of the morning. She got out of bed and caught Manny on the stairs.

"Your Veronica win, she take it all, she the Queen," he said.

The next morning they drove to the mas camp. All the other mas players had assembled by the time they got there. Esther looked for Jojo but he wasn't in the retinue of young men and women who helped the band on with their costumes.

Veronica looked beautiful. Esther wondered whether she had kept her costume on through the night, preening herself. Her eyes were now painted and the whites of them looked out of the tapestry of colour. Assembling the float and the players was a massive feat, or so it seemed to Esther. On this day there were ten men fussing around Veronica. Two stood by to help her carry the weight of her fantastic head-dress which stood three feet high and flowered like branches to the ground on either side. A young girl held the body of her flowing costume behind her.

The men in their steel band assembled themselves with a lot of fuss on the truck and there was some argument about whether the truck should precede the young dancers or follow it. There seemed to be hundreds of supporters and helpers milling around the camp, but when the show finally got on the road, order emerged from the confusion.

Jojo hadn't turned up. Esther realized that he wasn't just late; she had a feeling that he didn't want to be there. Claude and his friends were there, in jeans and sweat shirts with the word FANTASIA signed across them, obviously wanting to be identified as the creators of the band's visual splendours.

As the Fantasia of the Ethereal Air hit the road, the vision of its creators seemed to come alive, a still picture transformed to dance and laughter. There had to be music, there had to be the assembly of bodies in lines and circles, dancing in wave formation to the beat of the pansmen, the steady clacking of the two boys who got off the truck with pipes and sticks and stood among the dancers giving them the rhythm.

The float moved out of the side streets and on to Ladbroke Grove. Their band and its crowds were joined by others from different directions, all flowing into the main stream. As they paused at street corners, Esther watched them approaching and felt the thrill of being part of a massive plan, part of a purpose working itself out. She decided to take a moment to leave her band and try and spot Carol and Josie dancing in theirs. She said that to herself and at the same time realized that her eyes were sifting through the crowds for Jojo. Why had he stayed away? His mates had helped her on with her costume. It fitted perfectly. The wings were lighter than she had thought and Jojo had painted extra stars on them the night before. There were more mas players than she had expected. It was the biggest, the most graceful, the most soulful, their masquerade was *it*.

In the centre, thrusting to the front in a slow and dignified dance, as though she were balancing herself within the circle of dancers, went Veronica, conscious of the gasps from the crowd.

She was the slowest mover in the group. Her wings didn't flap, they gently undulated, like the great branches of a proud tree. The feathers on her head waved to the blue August sky, while all around her, like birds who sought her shelter, were the young ones, their bodies swaying to Soaky's encouragement.

For a while Manny walked next to Esther, who was all

smiles. Mistress Waters, in a blue Sunday dress, clutching her handbag, her eyes glinting with pride, walked next to him.

Esther had never seen so many people gathered together in her life. The streets were human for the day. No cars, no commerce, it seemed to her, only people and their clamour . . . not only the music and the shouts of encouragement, but the arguments and the comments. Everyone seemed to Esther to have fallen under the spell of the performance. There were no spectators, there seemed to be no one who stood aloof.

There were so many white faces, so many thousands of black faces. As Esther danced, she kept her eye on Manny, on her mother, walking among the crowded throng on the pavement. She herself was in the charmed circle, the space made for those who had prepared, the respectful ten square feet of empty road that moved in the wake of the truck which looked now like a boat cutting through water, pushing ripples of the crowd to the side.

Still no Jojo. The procession wound its way under the railway arch of the Grove and turned down towards Portobello Road. To Esther it was unfamiliar territory, streets she didn't know, but in the whirl of the dance it seemed to her that they were streets she possessed. Dancing was like floating above the crowd and moving like a spaceship, and yet it was also like stamping the earth, pounding the road and making it yours with your footsteps. There were delays. The band halted, the truck stopped moving. Young men, some boys she recognized from Brixton, thousands she hadn't seen before, surged forward in long lines, like human chains, across the street, through the dance and through the crowd. When their own band stopped, Esther could hear what seemed like a hundred other sounds. She turned and saw there was another band just behind them, and the sounds of reggae and the resounding insistence of beating pan came over the rooftops and down the streets. People had established themselves at the windows of the houses, with chairs on the balconies; people sat on the walls of the terraces; people everywhere, some still moving to the beat of distant sounds . . . the forward and backward motion of the calypso walk.

There were brief moments when Esther forgot about Jojo, stopped looking for him, paused to absorb herself in the masquerade. But somehow she couldn't keep him out of her festive head. Her eyes would turn and look at each group of young men as they passed one way and then the other. He should have been there to see what he had helped to create. He should have been with the Fantasia to see her carry her costume and herself. Last night she had thought that she would be dancing for him. He would walk and "chip" along with them, and she would show him that he shouldn't have called her "Cata"; she was no caterpillar, no crawling, infant thing; she was a beauty and she could float and she felt high.

The band moved off again. Soaky walked back through it and tried to keep the dispersed players together in a tight arrangement. He looked worried and he frowned. Manny got hold of his arm as Soaky passed and asked if everything was all right.

Soaky grasped him by the shoulder.

"It's a fucking police Carnival," Esther heard him say.

It was then that she saw them. How could she have missed them? Smiling bobbies all round, in the crowd but apart from it. As they moved off, they were forced to stop once more by a blue police van furrowing through, a group of six policemen walking in front of it to make way for it in the defiant crowd. Officers passed from group to group with instructions. She saw coppers in pairs talking to each other, standing like lamp-posts, part of the furniture of the streets. They leaned forward, bending their heads to lend their ears to people who asked them for directions. Esther forgot about them when their float moved on and Veronica climbed on to the back of the truck and sat down to take a rest, arranging her costume about her, facing the dancers from the back of their float.

Every twenty yards the float would stop, the players would be joined by by-standers and the steel band would rise to new heights of noisy performance. At the top of the "'bello", among a crowd of young men and women on a platform, Esther saw Jojo. He was wearing a red, green and gold tam and a black shirt and suède trousers. She had never seen him look so fancy before. Behind him and his companions on the wooden platform, was a battery of loudspeaker boxes. She saw he was with some girls. They looked like rude girls to Esther.

She watched him and pretended not to be looking. Then he saw her. He was fifty yards away and a sea of people divided them. Esther knew he had seen the float, identified it and had spotted her. The next time she looked he was no longer on the platform. He had disappeared. She couldn't understand it. He had worked so hard. It would have been his day. In the days through the preparation of their mas, Esther had neglected the thought that he might have some other life, other friends. He had seemed so permanent in the camp. Every time she was there, he was. He seemed so respectful of Soaky, taking instructions from him, learning this and that about the designs, listening carefully when Soaky became all artistic and philosophic about the thing they were doing, and recalling the days in Trinidad when he had beat pan and danced and fought in the Caribbean sun.

So he had rude friends. So he could get out of his sweat-shirt which said "Harlem University" and his paint-

.eared jeans and his grubby beret, and become the nifty
ɔuth-man of Brixton, his own masquerade.

Soon the day would be over and she would find Manny
or he would find her and they would drive back and she
would keep her costume and he would forget about the care
he had taken over it; her mother would boast to Carol's
mother about how Esther had been part of the "boss" band
that year, and the mas camp would revert to being a hollow
wooden shell without the industry and the clamour, and she
wouldn't see Jojo again. The thought pinched something
inside her. Esther didn't want to dance any more. She was
suddenly thirsty and dry and her eyes didn't want to look up
at the faces, but only down now at the patches of road in
front.

She walked forward as they moved, and there he was
again. He pushed through the crowd and walked confidently
into the circle. Just behind him walked one of the girls
Esther had seen standing behind him on the platform. He
must be coming to greet Soaky, to meet his friends. No,
he was coming up to her. The girl behind him cast possessive
eyes on him, her manner saying that he was walking too
fast for her, pushing too far ahead through the difficult
crowd. Jojo extended his arms.

"How go, how go, how go?" he said to the other dancers,
who greeted him as he walked up.

"How you dancing, Cata?" he said to Esther and she
pretended not to have heard him, and bent down to adjust
the strap of her high-heeled shoe.

Esther watched him manoeuvre his way through the
dancers, up to the float, to the side of the truck, impatiently,
forcing the girl who was with him to follow. And then, a
few yards further, as she lost sight of him, he appeared
through the crowd again just by her side. He was smiling.
He expected Esther to appreciate the dodge he had pulled

on the girl who was following him. "We are going to play all day, all night, all the Carnival year round!"

Esther's eyes searched for the girl, but Jojo had lost her. If that was his girl-friend, why had he left her?

"I been looking for you all morning."

"You knew where we started."

"Yeah, yeah, but I had a lickle work."

"I saw your work."

Jojo grinned. The pansmen started beating again, a slow, lilting rhythm. Now that the lilt of the dance had gone out of her body, Esther felt low, felt abandoned by the spirit that made people jam together. She even felt a bit absurd. She had planned to say to him that she liked the new stars he'd put on the costume, she was grateful for the best costume amongst the young dancers, but all that slipped her mind. In front of that girl he had called her by that name again. That was his woman; she was only "Cata".

Esther blinked to push back the liquid which seemed to seep into her lower eyelids. She pushed past Jojo, who was walking backwards now, facing her. She made for the edge of the crowd to push her way through it.

"What go on?" he shouted after her.

His hand was on her shoulder and she turned to look full in his face.

"I'm very thirsty, I've been dancing hours, I need a drink."

"Claude will get you a drink," he said, but she was already pushing her way through the crowd.

Behind it there was an edge of pavement along which she could walk. People stared at her as she walked in her costume along the shop fronts, against the grain of the movement.

Esther turned down a side street, not quite knowing where she was going, and as she turned the corner, she moved her head ever so slightly to see if Jojo was following her. That would be the test. Did he care at all for her? His mocking and his sarcasm; she was sure that there was more feeling for her in him than that. She couldn't see him. She began to run now, down a clear street. She turned down another one. Here the crowd was thinner, but clusters of boys and girls stood in the middle of it, like teams of players in a field before a game.

At the next street corner there were three police cars and farther down the street a blue van full of policemen. Esther saw a crowd of people outside what looked like a restaurant, a table set out in front of it under an awning, selling Cokes and other drinks. She headed for it. Then she remembered she had no money. There was no pocket in her costume in which she could keep any. She paused in front of the stall.

"What you doing away from your troupe?" an old black man said, coming up to her.

"I came for a drink, a Coke," Esther said. "I've danced all through and I tired now."

"Shouldn't get tired, Carnival go on forever," the man said and he pranced on his old haunches. Then he put his arm in a grandfatherly way on her shoulders and said, "Coke no good for yuh, rot your teeth, you want to keep them sharp, little daughter." Esther laughed.

"Come in here," the old man said, "the mas must have its dues, come for a drink, nuh?" He motioned her with him into the restaurant.

It was crowded with black men and a few women. The man pushed his way authoritatively through the crowd and took Esther to the counter at the far end.

"I'm exhausted now. You don't notice when you're dancing, but it's so hot."

"Now you notice, it's right, it's right," the old man said and cleared a bench for her and made her sit down. It was

122

then Esther noticed that her feet ached and she was glad of the rest, and glad of the tall iced glass of pineapple juice that the old man placed before her.

He asked Esther her name, he said he knew Soaky, he said he knew it was the best band in town and said he was going to wear a sailor suit but his wife gave it away because she said he was too old to make a fool of himself. Esther said he was not too old and the man said he agreed that you were never too old.

"All are fit," he said, "you are never too old for each other," and he cast a glance from his wrinkled but laughing eyes. Sometimes you're too young, Esther thought. That was probably why Jojo didn't take her seriously. That's why he'd asked Manny her age. Until then he'd made her feel so much older than she was, made her forget her impatience to grow up.

The dark shade of the restaurant was suddenly open to daylight. In the doorway stood a group of policemen. The officer asked that nobody move. The crowd pushed against the tables as the heavy men in blue moved through them and went down the stairs to the basement. As soon as the coppers had passed, the restaurant emptied. The old man went with a bunch, following the policemen down to the basement. Esther was almost alone. The people had drained out into the streets. She could hear a clamour in the road outside. She rushed out. She must get back to the mas; she must at least get back to the shelter of the swarms and crowds.

As she stepped out of the door, she took in the scene. Two lines of policemen had formed a cordon and were moving slowly down the road with dustbin lids held in front of them. Behind them a policeman in an armoured car was looking over the phalanx at the crowd of black youth who were hurling bottles and cans and anything that came to hand.

123

ɔm the other end of the street, behind the throng of youth
ɔme six more police cars, their sirens going, and squads of
ɔue uniforms wedged into the crowds.

Esther was going back into the doorway, when the line of
policemen charged with savage shouts. Some of the youth in
the throng turned to run and others stood their ground,
hurling abuse. Still the barrage of tins came at the police
line. There were bottles smashing all over the street and
people screaming. Hysteria. Esther felt the panic grip her
stomach. Then she saw Jojo. One of the policemen at the
end of the line had grabbed him and was grappling with
him. The policeman kept calling to the others for help but
none of them approached that scuffle because they had their
hands full. The lines of confrontation broke into hand-to-
hand fights. Esther felt a rush of blood behind her ears
which told her she was beyond being afraid.

She rushed forward. The policeman had his arm around
Jojo's throat and Jojo's legs were attempting to get round
the policeman's to trip him. Together they looked like a
tripod that was whirling, unbalanced. Esther didn't notice
any of the other fighters. She threw herself blindly at the
policeman's arm and tugged at it. She didn't know what she
was doing. She opened her mouth and sank her teeth into
the arm, wild to get through the thick blue fabric. The
policeman shouted, but wouldn't loosen his grip and Esther
glimpsed Jojo's grin beneath his grimace of suffocation.

Esther lifted her mouth and screamed at the copper and
pounded her fists on his side.

Jojo seemed to be wrenching his neck loose from the lock.

"Behind," he shouted, and Esther felt a hand grab her by
the bicep and firmly fling her away from the scuffle. Two
policemen had come up behind her. She stumbled on her
heels, flung ten feet into the confused roadway. She got to her
feet and her instinct was to rush back into the fight. As soon

as she'd gathered her vision, she saw that Jojo had been subdued. He was on his knees with two policemen wrenching both his arms backwards. And yet he was smiling.

"Don't come," he shouted at Esther and he grinned broadly. "Take off, butterfly! Go on . . . spread it . . . We free!"

ABOUT THE AUTHOR

Farrukh Dhondy was born in Poona in India, went to school and college there and came to Britain to go to university.

He says: 'I always wanted to tell stories, to show off with words and incidents and perceptions rather than with footballs and cricket bats'.

He came to England to study, and turned into a sort of professional student as he was at different universities for six years – Cambridge, Leicester and, much later, York.

He worked as a school teacher in London for many years and then quit to write full time.

He still writes and now works as a Commissioning Editor of Multicultural Programmes for Channel 4, which he enjoys.